Susan looked up as Drew spoke to her

'I suppose you'd like to hear a report from the Flying Doctor service on our patient?'

A polite affirmation rose to her lips. . .and died there as it was overtaken by the anger and helplessness she had been bottling inside her all day.

'No, Drew, I wouldn't.' She had startled him, that was clear. 'I want to hear the truth about you and Simon.'

Dear Reader

Although our heroines have quite serious problems this month, we accentuate the positive, and show that even in the darkest hours we should not lose hope that there will be light at the end of the tunnel. And Christmas is coming—how could we be sad about that? Stay cheerful!

The Editor

!!!STOP PRESS!!! If you enjoy reading these medical books, have you ever thought of writing one? We are always looking for new writers for LOVE ON CALL, and want to hear from you. Send for the guidelines, with SAE, and start writing!

Lilian Darcy is Australian, but on her marriage made her home in America. She writes for theatre, film and television, as well as romantic fiction, and she likes winter sports, music, travel and the study of languages. Hospital volunteer work and friends in the medical profession provide the research background for her novels; she enjoys being able to create realistic modern stories, believable characters, and a romance that will stand the test of time.

Recent titles by the same author:

CONFLICTING LOYALTIES
RUNNING AWAY

A FATHER'S LOVE

BY

LILIAN DARCY

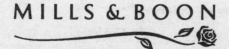

MILLS & BOON

MILLS & BOON LIMITED
ETON HOUSE, 18–24 PARADISE ROAD
RICHMOND, SURREY, TW9 1SR

MILLS & BOON, the Rose Device and LOVE ON CALL are trademarks of the publisher.

First published in Great Britain 1994
by Mills & Boon Limited

© Lilian Darcy 1994

Australian copyright 1994   Philippine copyright 1994
This edition 1994

ISBN 0 263 78854 7

Set in 10 on 10½ pt Linotron Times
03-9411-60129

Typeset in Great Britain by Centracet, Cambridge
Made and printed in Great Britain

CHAPTER ONE

SUSAN CARSTAIRS had a chronic disease, and there ought to be a name for it, but there wasn't. She was always early for appointments. It went beyond mere punctuality. Today, for example, she was supposed to be meeting Dr Drew Kershaw at this Collins Street café at four, and now it must be all of half-past three, if she was lucky.

She pushed up the sleeve of her tan raincoat and looked at the plain little watch on her left wrist. Twenty-four minutes past. Oh, well. . . I should be used to it by now. Why on earth didn't I bring a book? she thought.

Autumn rain was teeming down, making Melbourne's city streets look like grey rivers, and Susan's stockings were already uncomfortably wet around the ankles after the walk from the tram. The prospect of waiting for Dr Kershaw here outside the café door did not appeal. That wind off Port Phillip Bay was decidedly chilly on her damp legs.

'But if I go in and sit down, will he be able to work out who I am?' she thought anxiously.

Rendezvous in cafés and restaurants always made her anxious. It was one of the many legacies of her unhappy childhood, and as she stood just inside the café's entrance—dry at last!—the memories came flooding back. . .

Eccentric Aunty Dot used to escort her to just this sort of busy, anonymous place to meet her father for a snatched lunch during one of his business trips from Perth. A long wait invariably followed their arrival— Aunty Dot had been the one to infect Susan with her always-early disease. During those waits there had always been that sinking, horrible fear that he would not come and, on at least three occasions that she could remember, he hadn't. Then, after Aunty Dot went off to do some shopping, had come the lunch itself.

And, not surprisingly, it was always their last lunch together that Susan remembered best— the one that had come just a few days after Aunty Dot's funeral six years ago when Susan was seventeen. For once, she *hadn't* spent the meal biting her nails as she racked her brains for stories to tell Dad that would kindle a spark of love and interest in his eyes. Instead, he had been the one to break the silence.

'Sue. . .you know you have a home with us in Perth now if you want one.' The words had dragged from him, his reluctance painfully obvious. He had his new wife Kirsty now, and their pretty, golden-haired little girls, aged two and four.

'I don't think that's really a good idea, Father,' she had said very slowly. 'Aunty Dot left me the house. . .' And, for all the old woman's shortcomings as a guardian, she had provided a love of sorts after Susan's mother's death and her father's abandonment twelve years before, and the little house in one of Melbourne's older suburbs was the only home Susan now remembered. 'I've already enrolled to study nursing next February after I leave school, so I think it would be best if I stayed here.'

She would never forget the relief she had seen in his eyes. Shortly after this visit, the demands of his business had changed, and he'd no longer come to Melbourne. The token Christmas cards still passed back and forth. No presents any more. She wondered what he had done with the *papier mâché* pen-tray, the clumsily knitted socks, and the other half dozen items that an adoring little girl had so carefully made over the years. It was six years now since she had seen him, and five years since she had given up biting her nails. . .

'Look, are you waiting for me?' came an impatient voice, breaking the flood of memories. 'I've had to tap you on the shoulder twice.'

'Oh!' For a moment Susan was completely flustered, then she remembered that she *wasn't* here to see her father, and she wasn't ten or twelve or seventeen any more. She was twenty-three, a highly competent and well-regarded nurse, and about to embark upon an exciting new job that had more than a little adventure attached. 'Dr Drew Kershaw?' she said, and caught his brief nod. 'Yes, I *am* looking for you! Sorry I was in a daze. You're early too.'

'Well——' he looked at his watch '—I suppose I *was* a little early. It's just half-past three now.'

The comment didn't quite make sense to Susan since she was positive that their rendezvous had been arranged for four, but she let the matter slide and followed him to a table at the back, gathering her impressions as she went.

Firstly, he didn't seem to be in a very good mood. The shoulders on that medium-sized, athletic-looking frame were set very squarely and tightly, she saw as she studied his straight back. He hadn't smiled at her at all, and that made the planes of his face look longer, the cheekbones higher, the slightly freckled nose straighter and that well-drawn mouth very firm and unyielding. Dark brown hair fell over his high forehead in a couple of wayward locks, and beneath them she had seen that he frowned. So much for punctuality. Usually someone was angry if you were late to meet them, not if you were early!

He sat down and raised an assured hand to summon the waitress, who moved towards their table immediately. 'I've got someone else coming at four,' he told Susan. 'So let's order straight away, shall we? Coffee?'

'Espresso, please,' she said firmly. Aunty Dot had never permitted her to drink coffee, but over the past six years she had developed a defiant love for brews that were inky dark and strong.

'Two espressos, then,' Dr Kershaw told the waitress. He smiled at *her* very faintly, revealing extremely even white teeth, but when he turned back to Susan he was frowning again and his vividly green eyes were narrowed.

I hope I'm going to like this job, she thought, in her first moment of doubt about the new direction her life was about to take. After all, it'll just be the two of us. . .

A tiny town called Coolacoola in the outback—cattle country—of Western Australia, a new national park and a new mine in the Dymock Ranges bringing tourists, workers and families to the region, a brand-new medical centre. . . And Sister Susan Carstairs and Dr Drew Kershaw staffing it together and living in the two specially constructed houses that adjoined the medical centre building, set right in the middle of wild desert terrain. She had a calm conviction that she was going to find the place and the job very satisfying. But the company. . .?

'Now,' he said, taking some papers out of the expensive brown leather briefcase he carried. 'The school where you trained has given you a very good reference, as has your first employer, where you stayed for three years until the youngest child started school and you were no longer needed. This last job, though, you left after only six weeks, and I see that——'

'I'm sorry, Dr Kershaw!' Susan came in desperately. 'There's been some mistake. That's not my employment history you're describing. I've never done private nursing. I've been working at Richland Hospital since I finished my training and——'

'Nursing?' he came in, his face in a grimace of impatient confusion now. 'Wait a minute! Then you're Susan, not——' he glanced down at the papers in front of him '—Kylie Radbone.'

'No. . . I mean, yes, I'm Susan Carstairs.'

'You're early,' he accused.

'I told you I was.'

He sighed. 'And my prospective nanny is late. This is a nuisance!'

'Nanny?'

'Yes. I might as well tell you. My four-year-old son will be coming up to Coolacoola to live as well.'

'Oh, then you're married,' Susan said, quite pleased at the fact. It might be nice to have another woman around. Not to mention the nanny.

'No, I'm *not* married,' he corrected in a hard tone. 'I said my son. Nothing about a wife. And this has all happened at short notice, so——Ah!'

He rose and waved across the crowd of café tables. Following his gaze, Susan saw a bouncy blonde of about her own age craning a pretty head to study the café's occupants. Catching sight of Dr Kershaw's signal, the girl's brow cleared, she waved back, and began to make her way over.

'I'm sorry, Dr Kershaw,' she said brightly. 'The trams are running late today. I suppose it's the heavy rain. . .'

Susan, who had allowed an extra half-hour for late trams and heavy rain, was not particularly impressed with the excuse, but Drew Kershaw let it slide. He also waved away Susan's offer to go and sit at another table while he conducted the interview.

'You'll be seeing quite a bit of each other, I imagine, so stay. As long as Kylie doesn't mind.'

'It's fine,' the young woman assured them cheerfully.

So Susan sat there, sipping at her espresso very slowly and trying to look as if she wasn't listening. This was impossible, of course. She heard every word. From the beginning, it seemed as if Drew Kershaw had made up his mind to give Miss Radbone the job. Perhaps he felt he was running out of time. After all, they were due to fly up to Coolacoola on Monday, just five days away.

He conducted the interview quite competently and conscientiously, however, asking the young woman about the amount of first-aid training that her nanny school had provided, the time off she would expect, her experience with four-year-old boys, and her expectations of outback life.

'I'm going to love everything about it,' Kylie told him in answer to this last question. Susan had her doubts about this. She herself, for example, was not looking forward very much to the possibility of snakes. . .

Dr Kershaw also probed a little about why Miss Radbone had left her most recent position after only six weeks, and nodded at her explanation that the place was too far from public transport. Again, Susan felt that there was more to it than that, but it was only an intuition, and she couldn't really blame Drew Kershaw for accepting this answer at face value as well.

In short, it was a perfectly satisfactory interview, and Kylie Radbone seemed like a perfectly competent and well-qualified nanny.

But there's something missing, Susan thought. Missing in him. And I don't know what it is.

At five minutes to four Miss Radbone had departed, in possession of the new nannying job and keen to begin packing.

'Your little boy. . .?' Susan began questioningly to Dr Kershaw.

'Simon,' his father supplied reluctantly.

'Simon must be looking forward to all this enormously.'

Drew Kershaw's green eyes met Susan Carstairs' brown ones very deliberately. 'I suppose so,' he said. 'I haven't seen him for three months.'

Then he sat back, waiting for his new nurse's response and wondering just why he had felt such a perverse need to cast himself in the worst possible light as a father. To cut corners, he supposed, noting her open-mouthed exclamation of surprise, quickly suppressed, and the ensuing silence that radiated a disapproval she barely troubled to try and hide. She was bound to reach the conclusion that he was a bad father eventually. Why pretend at this stage?

His brother Charles and sister-in-law Kate didn't think he was a bad father, of course. Having looked after the child with all the love he could possibly want since he was fourteen months old, they still made allowances for Drew's neglect. He could almost see empathic Kate thinking sometimes, Poor Drew, even after three years, it still grieves him too much to be with Simon, and to look at him. He *does* look so much like Lisa, too, more so every day.

Drew also knew that Charles and Kate thought he should be doing more to get over Lisa's death by this time. They were very much in favour of this new job, which would take him away from Melbourne and memories. And now Kate was pregnant at last, after six years of waiting. The fertility treatments had been almost *too* successful, in fact, and she was expecting triplets. Four months into the pregnancy, she was already uncomfortable and her obstetrician had recently warned her that she should expect to begin complete bed-rest any day now—something that was quite incompatible with caring for an energetic four-year-old boy.

'I *can't* risk losing these babies,' she had told Drew a week ago with tears in her voice. 'Not after waiting so long. I know how hard it is for you, and we'll miss him terribly, but. . .isn't it time you took Simon?'

And Drew had known that, in the eyes of the world, and of everyone who cared about him, it was.

'I suppose Simon has been living with his mother, has he?' Susan Carstairs was asking brightly. Drew knew that she was only trying to make innocent conversation, but he couldn't help the growl that escaped his lips.

'His mother is dead.'

'Oh. . . I'm sorry,' she whispered, and he knew he had made her feel clumsy and tactless. He wondered what she would do if he told her the truth—that the only emotion he felt towards Lisa now was anger.

This meeting today in order to get to know each other wasn't going too well. He shouldn't have tried to streamline his schedule by fitting in that too sketchy nanny interview as well, but he knew he had done so because he wasn't letting himself think too much about the reality of having the boy to live with him after all this time. He had been forced to hire a nanny, he had now hired one, and that was that. For the moment he could push the matter aside and concentrate on the new job. . .and Susan Carstairs.

'So tell me about yourself, Susan,' he said, and studied her as he listened—or half listened—to her reply.

'Well, I'm twenty-three,' she began.

In some ways she looked older. Perhaps this was because she didn't look particularly happy. But there was a youthful innocence to her face as well, and that might come from its complete lack of make-up, and from the rather nondescript cut of her medium-brown hair. She had brown eyes, overly pale skin and a generous scattering of freckles, and the tan blouse and skirt she wore did nothing to brighten this colouring. Why didn't Miss Susan Carstairs try to make more of herself? For no good reason, the matter angered him.

Belatedly, he realised that her eyebrows, innocent of any plucking, were extremely well-drawn, arching over those chocolate-coloured eyes with a faint questioning look, and that her mouth was a perfect pale pink bow.

Smile, damn it! he wanted to tell her suddenly. Then he listened more closely to what she was saying.

'So I've been living in that little house alone since

Aunty Dot died. It's a long way from the hospital and it turned out to need a fair bit of expensive mainten-ance—a new roof, among other things—so I haven't had much time or money for friends and going out, and I finally realised that it wasn't doing me any good. I've just finished paying for the roof, and I decided I should either get another nurse in to share the place with me, or rent it out, apply for a job elsewhere and get to see something of Australia. The second possibility sounded *much* more interesting!'

She *did* smile at last, and the effect was magic. It was an elfin, mischievous smile that parted those pretty lips, raised the questioning eyebrows even further and set her brown eyes all a-twinkling. 'Ah. . .!' said Drew.

'I mean——' the smile faded and she grew hesitant and close-faced once again '—I presume that's what you were really asking me, isn't it? Why I wanted the job? Sorry it took me so long to get to the point.'

'That's all right,' he answered absently.

'And now, what about you?'

Susan tried to infuse the question with some of Kylie Radbone's effervescence, but it didn't work. For one thing, bubbles and giggles weren't her style. For another, she already detested Drew Kershaw. He seemed a sour sort of man and she regretted that she had betrayed so much to him about her lack of family and her loneliness and struggles in Melbourne—regret-ted it, even though she sensed he hadn't fully been listening.

His face had worn the angry expression she had first seen when he'd approached her in the café entrance, and she had begun to suspect that it was a semi-permanent fixture. Don't you know how to smile? She wanted to ask him suddenly, interrupting his bland, careful account of why his job running the casualty department at one of Melbourne's biggest hospitals no longer satisfied him.

Not smiling enough was the least of his sins, though.

It was that icy statement about his son that really set the seal on her feelings. 'I haven't seen him for three months.'

Three months! To a child, three months was a lifetime. She knew this from her own experience only too well, and he had offered no excuse for his neglect. Where was the child now? she wondered. And did Drew Kershaw know how harshly most people would judge him for his attitude? He certainly didn't seem to care.

'We ought to talk about our timetable for opening up the place,' he was saying now. 'We have three changes of plane on Monday, and the last one is a tiny thing that makes mail-drops at every cattle station along the route, so we won't arrive until pretty late. My plan is to spend Tuesday settling in and exploring our set-up. Supposedly some bureaucratic branch of the Western Australian Health Department has organised supplies, and the centre is fully equipped, but you never know. If everything *is* in order, then I'd like to open for business on Wednesday. It's only by actually starting to see patients that we'll be able to assess whether things are working.'

'So. . .'

'Yes, a tight schedule. But of course I don't know how much Simon may complicate our plans.'

Suddenly, Susan's anger rose in her throat like bile. Her voice, though, was coldly polite. 'If he's going to be such a nuisance, I wonder why you're bringing him.'

They glared at each other, his hostility as apparent now as her own.

'I have no choice but to bring him,' Drew hissed darkly. 'Believe me, I'd rather not.'

'That must be making Simon look forward to the change.'

'Don't be ridiculous! Do you think I'd tell him how I feel about it?'

'Do you think a child *needs* to be told?' Her tone,

low and vibrant, was a threatening parody of his. 'A child's emotional sense is ten times sharper than an adult's. Believe me, he'll know how you feel!'

For several moments he did not reply, but, daring to study him more boldly in her anger, Susan saw that his square jaw was tightly clenched and a small muscle beat in a tense rhythm beside his mouth. Had she gone too far? At the moment, she didn't care.

'If we are to work together amicably in a very isolated place,' he said at last, 'you will kindly not comment on personal matters in my life that are none of your concern.'

His green eyes were as cold as glacial ice, and his lips were drawn into a thin, hard line. She returned his gaze unflinchingly, her anger against him more than a little infused with the anger at her father that she had never been able to express.

'Of course,' she said at last. 'It would make working together impossible, wouldn't it? And, having made this big change in my life, I want it to work out, so from now on, as you say, your personal life is none of my concern. I won't comment again.'

'But whether you comment or not, you'll go on thinking the same way. That's what you're implying, isn't it?' he demanded now.

'Yes, it is,' she nodded, feeling two spots of colour burning on her cheeks, but holding her head high.

'Did it ever occur to you that there might be complexities to my relationship with Simon that you know nothing about?'

'Complexities?' she returned at once. 'Yes, adults are very good at finding complexities in a situation that seems only too simple to a child.'

'Enough!' His hard fist, thumping on the table with barely reined violence, made her jump and flinch back in her seat with a gasp. 'I won't be drawn into this discussion.' He had lowered his voice, aware of stares from neighbouring tables, but the fact that his words were audible only to her seemed to make them even more menacing. 'If we weren't flying to Coolacoola on Monday, I'd attempt to have you replaced. As it is——'

He stopped abruptly. She was frightened by his anger, he could tell, and yet she still met his gaze steadily with those brown eyes. Her chin was tilted defiantly upwards, showing a beautifully drawn jawline and a very slender, graceful neck. There was something quite courageous in the way the plain little miss had spoken out about what she felt and believed, and suddenly, most unexpectedly, he craved her good opinion.

'Look,' he said, his tone more gentle and almost beseeching now, although he regretted each word almost before it had been spoken, 'don't think too harshly of me on this issue. Believe me, the whole thing is a struggle for me and sometimes I'm not sure. . .if I'll ever manage to do the right thing. Let's leave it, OK? I should go, and I'll see you at the airport on Monday.'

'Yes. It's an early flight, isn't it?' she managed.

'Eight o'clock, I believe. You're not in the habit of missing planes, I hope!'

'No, I'm not,' she laughed. Late? She would probably arrive at the airport before it opened. Or did airports stay open all the time? 'At least. . .' she went on. 'Actually, I've never flown before.'

He raised his dark eyebrows, clearly taken aback at the admission and floored as to a response. She helped him out, since he had already said that he needed to go. 'I'm looking forward to the adventure, though. . . and I'll see you on Monday,' and he left quickly after echoing the polite phrase.

Susan stayed on and ordered another espresso. She was far more drained by this meeting with Drew Kershaw than she had expected to be, especially that last part. His anger had been as deeply rooted as her own, hinting at drama and tragedy in his past, just as hers had hinted at neglect and loss. Then had come that evidence of vulnerability at the end, so totally unexpected that she hadn't responded to it at all, and was left now with a rapidly beating heart, pink cheeks, anger, curiosity, and a silly desire to cry.

'I'll see him. . .and Simon. . .and Kylie Radbone on Monday,' she murmured aloud, then took a bite of her butterfly cake. 'I hope we manage to be cooler about it all then.'

'Susan?'

'Hello,' she squeaked at Drew, heroically suppressed excitement raising the pitch of a voice that was normally very resonant and of a surprisingly mature depth.

'You haven't checked in already?' he said.

'Yes, I. . .' The punctuality problem again. She had been the very first one in line after the check-in counter opened for her flight.

'Let's hope we'll be able to sit together, then.'

'Oh, of course. I didn't think. I should have waited.'

'Never mind. We're still pretty early. I'll check in now—I have Simon and Kylie's tickets as well—and ask that they be given the two seats behind us or across the aisle, if they're still available.'

'I've got a window-seat,' Susan offered. 'Perhaps I can swap with Simon. That way he can have you beside him and a window as well.'

'Hmm.' Without further comment, he turned to the counter and spoke to the clerk there, stepping away a few minutes later to tell Susan, 'Keep your window-seat, since it's your first flight. I've got two seats directly behind us for Simon and Kylie, so he'll have a window.'

What? You don't even want to sit next to your son on a plane? Susan wanted to say to him. On Wednesday he had asked her, with that unsettling vulnerability, not to judge him, but already she found it difficult.

'Kate and Charles should be arriving with Simon at any minute,' he was saying now. 'We arranged to meet just here. . . Ah!'

Susan followed his gaze and saw a couple and a child coming towards them. Simon and his foster-parents? Evidently not.

'My brother Charles and his wife Kate, with whom Simon has been living for the past three years,' Drew explained as they approached.

Charles Kershaw was a slightly older, slightly plumper version of his brother, with fair hair and grey eyes instead of green ones. Red-headed Kate looked petite and pretty in a pale blue polo-neck and darker over-dress that betrayed but flattered her pregnancy. Beside them, holding Kate Kershaw's hand, walked small Simon. . .

Susan's heart went out to the child instinctively. He broke away from his uncle and aunt as soon as he saw Drew, and ran up to him. 'Daddy! Daddy!' His face, now that it was smiling, was uncannily like Drew's in expression, although his colouring was fair, his skin without freckles and his eyes blue.

'Hello, Simon.' At first, Drew simply put out a hand and pressed it on the small boy's shoulder, then, slowly and with almost tangible reluctance, he lifted the eager child into his arms and gave him a stiff, quick embrace.

The pinched expression of disappointment on Simon's face made Susan's throat tighten, and her own features felt strained as she thought about how often that look must have appeared on her own face as a child. Hating Drew Kershaw again, she noticed that Simon did not look nearly so much like his father when his face was closed and set like that. It was laughter and pleasure that brought out the unmistakable Kershaw features, which were repeated so clearly in Charles's face as well.

'Kate, aren't you supposed to be in bed?' Drew said,

turning to scold his sister-in-law as soon as he had put Simon down.

'I had to come and wave my precious boy away on the aeroplane,' she answered, her arm already around the child's shoulders in an instinctive gesture of comfort and love.

'I'm going to be living with Daddy in the desert,' Simon informed everyone unnecessarily. 'But it's not going to be just me and him.' His frowning glance took in Susan uncertainly, as she stood beside Drew.

'No, it's not,' Drew Kershaw answered his son with false heartiness. 'Simon, this is Sister Carstairs, who is a nurse. She's going to help me look after sick people at Coolacoola.'

'Sister Casters,' the little boy attempted.

'Would you like to call me Susan?' She exchanged a quick glance with Drew and received his nod of approval at the suggestion.

To Simon, 'Susan' was clearly a vast improvement. He turned eagerly to Kate. 'Susan! I know that name! My friend Ben's *pig* is called Susan!'

His tone made it evident to everyone that to have the same name as Ben's pig was to be blessed indeed, and the human owner of the name had to suppress a bright laugh as she caught the twinkling eyes of the other adults, including Drew's very green-eyed gaze.

'Let's get you checked in, Simon,' the latter said gruffly, as if regretting that he had allowed his son to give him a moment of pleasure and amusement.

'Checked in?' The little boy looked doubtful as he saw the parade of luggage moving towards a rubber curtain at the end of the conveyor belt behind the service desks.

'Not you, Simon, love,' Kate said gently, squeezing his arm. 'Your luggage. Don't worry, you'll be sitting with Daddy.'

'With Miss Radbone, actually,' Drew came in

abruptly. 'Kylie. Your nanny, Simon. Susan and I have work to do on the flight.'

Susan glanced at him, surprised. This was the first she had heard of it. She hadn't thought there was anything they had to do until they reached Coolacoola. It was just another excuse not to sit next to the boy, she realised in disgust, and gave Dr Kershaw a scathing look which caught him full in the face.

At that moment, Kylie Radbone herself came bouncing up to the group, her luggage consisting of a battered backpack, an old brown suitcase, and two plastic shopping bags. She wore her blonde hair in a mass of tiny plaits threaded with bright beads, and her outfit of big baggy shorts in a tropical print and a sleeveless cotton singlet-top in vivid orange looked more appropriate for the beach than for a long day of flying.

Introductions were made quickly, and Susan saw that Charles and Kate both looked a little ill at ease at the sight of Simon's nanny, although Simon himself did not yet seem to have taken in the fact that he would be spending much of his time at Coolacoola with this stranger, instead of with his adored father.

'We can't put all my luggage in the cargo,' Simon said, now that it had been explained to him what and where the cargo hold was. 'I need my magic goody bag with me on the plane.'

'Don't tell me *you* have a magic goody bag as well, Simon!' Kylie said with a chirp, and it turned out that the two plastic shopping bags contained toys, books and games—one bag for the flight, one for 'when we get there.'

Kate and Charles looked very relieved as the little boy and his new nanny began a lively guessing game about what was in their respective bags, and Susan relaxed as well. Simon was giggling happily, and Kylie herself seemed to be enjoying the fun. Perhaps the nagging doubts she still had about the nanny's casual manner would prove unfounded, and Drew Kershaw's judgement in hiring her so quickly would be vindicated.

'We've got another half-hour before we need to board,' he said, after a frowning glance at the masculine silver wristwatch he wore. 'Do you want to leave straight away, Charles? Kate, do you need to rest? Or shall we all sit down and have a snack? You'd like an orange juice, wouldn't you, Simon? And perhaps a bun?'

'Yes, please!' Again, Susan saw the eager way Simon responded to any suggestion that came from his father.

There was general agreement to the plan in the end, although at first Charles did want to get Kate home to rest. They lived in Healesville, to the north-east of Melbourne, on two acres of land—a delightful place for Simon, but quite a distance from the airport, and they had had to make a very early start.

'I can rest over orange juice,' Kate insisted, then added firmly, 'And I'm feeling quite thirsty.' But the real reason, Susan could clearly see, was that she didn't want to leave Simon until the last possible moment.

Whether deliberately or by accident, the pregnant woman fell into step beside Susan as they made their way to the cafeteria. Drew and Charles were ahead, deep in conversation about one of Charles's patients— he was also a doctor—while Simon tried manfully to keep up with his father, his small, denim-clad legs working busily. Kylie—again Susan noted the fact with relief—was just behind the boy, keeping him closely in view.

'I must say,' Kate said abruptly in a low tone to Susan, as if only waiting until she felt sure that none of the others was listening, 'Miss Radbone doesn't look like quite what I was hoping for.'

'No, perhaps not,' she agreed helplessly, very sympathetic to this pleasant-faced woman's obvious anxieties.

'For a start,' Kate Kershaw went on, 'I expected her

to be older, more motherly. More *serious* I suppose. She looks so frivolous, don't you think?'

'Her references were good. . .'

'Look, I'll be blunt. I worry about Simon a lot and——'

'Please,' Susan said in her usual careful way, 'you don't have to explain. It's obvious that Dr Kershaw's relationship with his son is. . .complicated.'

'Has he talked much about it to you?'

'No, not much,' she admitted. 'But he mentioned that he hadn't seen Simon for three months, and that made it pretty clear to me that something was wrong.'

'Poor Drew,' Kate said, surprising Susan.

Evidently his sister-in-law didn't blame him for the estrangement. As she had at one point last Wednesday, she doubted her own harsh reaction to the situation, but then she hardened her heart. No matter how much love he received from Charles and Kate, Simon was still desperate to win the same degree of affection from his father, and if Drew Kershaw couldn't see that he must be blind. If he *could* see it, and didn't care, then he must be a monster!

'I have to ask this,' Kate was saying now. 'You look sensible and caring, and you obviously must be a good nurse or you wouldn't have got this job. That's worth more in my book than one of these three-month courses at a nanny school. Sister Carstairs. . .'

'Please call me Susan.'

'Susan, then. Charles and I have wanted a baby for six years, and I'm going to do everything I can to give these triplets a safe, healthy birth—including taking the complete bed-rest that my obstetrician recommends—but I'm worried that if Simon isn't happy up at Coolacoola nothing can be done about it.'

'Will you be able to come up for a visit at some stage?'

'Yes, we plan to, after the babies are born and as

long as everything goes well, but that'll be October, over six months away.'

'Mm, that is a while.'

'Can you write to me every now and then and tell me how things are going?'

'Of course. I'll try to do it often. And I'll keep a close eye on Kylie, too, if you want me to.'

'Thank goodness you're the sort of person who really knows and cares about what a child feels!' Kate exclaimed in a fervent tone that drew a questioning look from her husband, back over his shoulder. He turned away again without saying anything when he saw that Kate and Susan were immersed in women's talk.

Drew had heard the emphasis in Kate's tone as well, and his ears burned as he guessed that she was talking about himself and Simon. It was always painful to him to see Charles' and Kate's concern, and he had never managed to find a way to deal with it. He dreaded the pummelling his emotions were going to receive over the coming months. He had felt a wrenching twist of pain inside him when he'd held Simon in his arms a short while ago, part of him wanting to clutch the child to him and never let him go and the rest of him filled with the ever-present dread that if he gave in to that need he would only end up doing violence to the little boy somewhere down the line.

Drew remembered as vividly as if it were yesterday the murderous rage he had felt towards Craig Osborne the night Lisa had left to go with the other man, taking Simon with her. He remembered how, after they left, he had gone tearing through the house—he had sold it soon afterwards and moved to a flat—smashing ornaments and pounding at things with his fists, wishing that it were Craig himself at the other end of those abandoned, heedlessly destructive blows.

He had not lost control like that either before or since, but the fact that he—a doctor, caring, com-

passionate, professionally trained—was capable of such
animal rage and violence had terrified and appalled
him, and the fear that he might erupt against Simon in
the same way haunted him like a hideous shadowy
spectre.

It was only a few days after Lisa left him that she
and Craig had both been killed in a car accident.
Simon, miraculously, had survived unharmed. And so
the sordid, unspeakable things that Lisa and Drew had
said to each other as she'd packed her things to go with
Craig lived only in *his* memory now. Yes, they lived
there still, and vividly, although he had done everything he could to suppress them and shut them out. . .

When the news of the car accident had come, Kate
and Charles had quietly taken Simon up to
Healesville—'until you've sorted things out, Drew.'
They hadn't known why Lisa and the little boy were in
the car with Craig that night, and as the months had
passed Simon had stayed on in Healesville, while Drew
grieved—not, as Kate and Charles thought, for his lost
wife, but for the loss of something that had been far
more precious to him. . .

This morning, he was again aware of Susan Carstairs'
hostility and disapproval over his treatment of the boy,
and he wondered exactly what female confidences were
being exchanged behind him at this moment. It was
unfortunate that he and Charles had finished their
medical discussion and had lapsed into silence, since
those feminine voices—Kate had a lovely voice, and,
actually, so did little Miss Carstairs—impinged much
more strongly now.

Thank goodness they were almost at the cafeteria!
He had been pleased, though, to see how at ease Susan
immediately was with the child—even when she found
herself being flatteringly compared with a pig! He
smiled unwillingly and began to throw off his black
mood as he compared the little scene with the disas-

trous trip up to Healesville back in December to visit Kate, Charles and Simon.

That was the last time he had succesfully conquered his inner demons enough to see the child. For emotional camouflage, he had brought Angela Coombes, an attractive blonde resident at the hospital and, at the time, briefly, the woman in his life.

Dr Coombes had been far too keen—and too obvious about it, as well—to gain Simon's approval, and had descended upon the small boy in a cloud of sickly perfume, saying, 'Darling! Is that your dinosaur? Oh, he's so *adorable*, isn't he? Now, *do* give me a kiss!' Very different from Sister Carstairs.

Simon had not been impressed, and had said so, bluntly, in his high treble half an hour later. 'Does Daddy like you? *I* don't!'

He had been scolded for his rudeness, of course, but Drew had remembered the old saying about children and fools telling the truth and he didn't think that Angela was very surprised when he had stopped asking her out a couple of weeks later. In the best of circumstances, it didn't take much to put him off a woman these days, after the ghastly fiasco of his marriage to Lisa.

Now, as the group seated themselves around a table at the bland airport cafeteria, he reflected that Susan Carstairs, with the prim disapproval and dislike that was written all over those plain and very ingenuous features at this very moment, had the potential to cause some horrible problems at Coolacoola, but at least incurring Simon's dislike would surely not be one of them.

CHAPTER TWO

'As you can see, our airstrip is pretty impressive now,' said Tom Arnold, the red-bearded head ranger at Coolacoola National Park.

He had met their small plane, which was already preparing to take-off again along the straight strip of reddish bitumen. Its final hop of the day was to the mining camp of Jambarra twenty miles further into the bush. There, two hundred men lived an exclusively bachelor existence during demanding nine-day shifts before taking six-day breaks with their wives and families in the coastal town of Pendleton, about five hundred kilometres distant, or even as far away as Perth. Not surprisingly, the miners welcomed the thrice-weekly contact with the mail plane and its pilot.

Susan looked back at the windy strip and watched the plane gather speed for take-off. Simon was absorbed in the sight as well. He had slept for two hours on the way from Melbourne to Perth, then for part of the way from Perth to Pendleton as well, and was now refreshed and full of curiosity about everything he saw.

The wind tossed some red dust into Susan's hair and face from the smoothly graded section that ran beside the sealed strip, and she tried to fan it away, thinking, Hats from now on, it it's often windy like this.

The thought was echoed by Kylie in a rather whining tone. 'Is it always windy like this?'

'Out here on the airstrip, yes, mostly,' Tom Arnold nodded, his cheerful grin disappearing into his beard. He picked up Kylie's suitcase and backpack and dumped them unceremoniously into the back of his four-wheel drive. Susan saw that the vehicle was emblazoned with a national park logo on each side.

'Careful of my blow-drier!' Kylie said.

Drew was loading luggage as well, and Susan helped him by picking up Simon's small suitcase and toy-bag. Soon everyone had piled into the vehicle. Tom drove like an outback veteran, bouncing the squeaking machine over the smaller bumps and potholes and swinging the wheel sharply to avoid the worst ones. Kylie squawked several times and Simon screamed with delight at the bouncing, while Susan made another mental note: I'm going to have to work on my driving.

The journey from the open, lightly scrubby terrain surrounding the airstrip was a short one, only a mile or two, and in that time the landscape changed dramatically. Rusty brown piles of rock grew to become sharply sculpted hills slashed by deep gorges, and from one of the deepest emerged a dry riverbed filled with smoothly worn river pebbles and shaded by stately, white-trunked gum trees.

'How often does it run?' Drew asked the park ranger, gesturing at the wide bed.

'Once every ten years. . .or once a week.' Tom Arnold grinned again. 'Depends on the rains. We've had good ones over the past couple of years. Nearly flooded the ranger station last winter, but now we're getting back to normal—a dry bed, and deep water-holes up in the gorges that are great for swimming.'

A moment later, Susan saw Coolacoola. It could scarcely be called a town. First came a couple of houses and a petrol station, then a long, low motel building that was almost new. Susan counted ten identical doors in a row and noted that there was room for an extension. If the new national park was as beautiful and interesting as she had been told, then the enterprising owners of the place might be on to a good thing within the next few years. Attached to the motel was a tiny store.

'Surprising what Lee Shipton can sell you,' Tom commented, gesturing at it. 'Prices are outrageous, of course, but the Shiptons work hard at their place and they deserve to make a go of it.'

He had turned left into Coolacoola's one street, unsealed, that separated the town from the river, and now they passed four more houses, each less than a year old. Beyond these came another house, still under construction, that was attached by a walkway to an airy-looking building with a wide veranda and a floor-level raised several feet off the ground. An identical roofed walkway connected this building to a slightly larger house on the other side, and then came the ranger station and visitors' centre, clearly identified by a big wooden sign on the front that again displayed the park logo.

'So if this is the ranger station,' Susan realised, 'then this building next door with the house attached must be our medical centre.'

Wait a minute! House? It should be in the plural. . .

'Shame about your place, Sister Carstairs,' Tom Arnold flung at her over the back of the seat at that moment. 'But it won't take much longer. The building crew got snaffled by the mining camp to put in an extra recreation building for the men, and Minex International pays more than the government, so your house lost out for the moment. The builders say they'll be ready to start on it again next week, and after that it should go up in no time.'

'But. . .but where am I to live until then?' Susan asked in a small voice.

'Crikey!' He put on the brakes as he turned in front of the medical centre's one completed house and craned around to look at her. Beside him in the front seat, Drew Kershaw was frowning heavily. 'You don't mean to tell me they didn't let you know?'

'No, they didn't,' Drew came in heavily before Susan could speak.

'Bureaucrats!' was the park ranger's disgusted comment.

'They must have made some provisions for this,' Drew said. 'Can I ring Perth and——? No——' he looked at his watch. '——it's after five. The office I've been dealing with in the health department will be closed. We'll have to sort this out tomorrow. Meanwhile. . .'

The head ranger had switched off the idling motor now and opened the squeaky driver's side-door. Drew opened his own door, then paused with his fingers on the handle. 'Mine is a three-bedroom place, isn't it, Tom?'

'Yes, and pretty nice too, fitted out with everything you'll need, from what I've seen.'

'Susan, you'll have to stay with us,' the doctor finished.

Susan nodded quickly. What else could she do? The prospect didn't appeal, though. She was used to living alone, for one thing. For another, a quick calculation had told her that she and Kylie would be sharing a room, and the nanny had been getting on her nerves all day. But perhaps it would turn out to be only a temporary thing. Drew Kershaw was saying, still with that frown, 'They must have made some arrangement and forgotten to tell us. Room and board at the motel, perhaps.'

'There's the camping ground, too,' Tom Arnold offered. 'That's a couple of miles up Wingoona Gorge, and it has a few caravans available for rent.'

'A caravan. . .' Susan murmured. Being used to living alone was one thing, but getting shunted off by herself to a distant caravan in a strange place for the night—and possibly for weeks—was not a very cheering prospect.

Perhaps Dr Kershaw saw her tight expression. Or perhaps he was just sick of the subject. At any rate, he turned to her as they all waited for Tom Arnold to heft the luggage from the back of the vehicle, and said quite gently, 'Don't worry about it for tonight. We'll raise a stink if necessary. You won't get left out in the cold.' He touched her bare forearm lightly, and the imprint of his warm fingers sent an instant tingle down her spine.

'Thanks.' The word was blurred by the tightness in her throat.

She didn't know it, but Drew had almost volunteered to take that caravan himself. As they all walked up the front steps together, on to the veranda and through the unlocked front door into the new house, he shook his head in disbelief at the size of the entourage he had managed to collect. Two females of definitely marriageable age and a four-year-old boy who called him Daddy, when up until last week he had been living in bachelor solitude in a very pleasant flat. For three years that solitude had been utterly necessary to him, and he wasn't yet ready, he realised now, to give it up. Was he a fool to have taken this job?

He looked around. The place smelled of new paint and new carpeting, and was furnished in a bland, functionally cheerful manner that was designed to suit the succession of doctors—some married, some not—who would no doubt pass through over the coming years. He wondered how long he would end up staying. Might he still be here, as crusty and eccentric as some local desert lizard, at the end of his career? Or would it only be a year or two before he found the answer to questions about himself and his life that he hadn't even started to ask yet?

'Everything's switched on,' Tom Arnold was saying, 'so I'll leave you to explore and get settled. That is, unless there's anything else I can help you with. Jane likes my company at this time of day, and so do the kids. She's already stocked up the fridge a bit for you, and she'll be over later on with a casserole and a salad for your tea.' He used the traditional Australian expression for the evening meal.

Seeing that Drew was preoccupied with his thoughts, Susan stepped in and thanked the lanky head ranger for his help and the latter left. Kylie was wandering around aimlessly, fingering the mottled blue-grey fabric of the new couch, scuffing her foot across the square of carpet that filled much of the living-room. . .

'Ugh! New paint!' she said. 'What a revolting smell!'

'It's yucky,' Simon agreed in a very little voice.

There was a silence. Drew was still miles away. Both Kylie and Simon were looking at Susan, and in spite of his long sleep she could see that the little boy looked travel-weary, homesick and unhappy.

'It's yucky all right,' she said briskly and brightly. 'So let's get all these windows opened and let in some fresh desert air. Those river trees make everything look so cool, don't they?'

As she spoke, she slid the windows open on their aluminium runners and immediately a breeze came in and began to freshen the place. Insect screens kept flies at bay, and at night dark blue curtains would screen out moon and starlight that Susan suspected might be startlingly bright to city dwellers' eyes.

The fresh air helped Kylie and seemed to rouse Drew, but Simon still looked close to tears. Who could blame him? Kate and Charles were far away, the adventure of the aeroplane was over with, and now there was a strange house full of strange people to get used to.

'Come on, Simon,' Susan said to him, since Kylie didn't seem to be taking any initiative or responsibility at all, not to speak of Drew. 'Let's find your room.'

It wasn't hard. A corridor led to the three bedrooms, and the smallest, which had views of the river and the rocky hills beyond, contained one bed, sky-blue curtains with drawings of suns and trees and fences and cars, and a wall-frieze of native animals that clearly identified it as a child's room.

The bed was already made up with sheets and a light

wool blanket, and Susan knew that they probably had
Jane Arnold to thank for this. Wisely, she did not
suggest to Simon that they unpack all his things now,
but asked about the well-worn teddy-bear that had
accompanied the little boy on the plane.

'Is Ned-bear tired, do you think? He didn't sleep
much on the plane, did he?'

'No, he looked out of the window.'

'Then let's lay him down on the bed for a rest.'

'With Clown and Mustard,' Simon specified.

'Where are they, love, do you know? In this big
suitcase?'

'Yes, right on top. Aunty Kate made sure to put
them there because she knew they'd want to come out
straight away.'

With bear, clown and lion all arranged on the bed
and the windows in this room opened as well, it began
to seem just a little less new and strange to Simon, and
Susan saw his expression relax and brighten. Seizing
her opportunity, she said at once, 'Now we have to go
outside.'

'Why?'

'Because there might be treasures to find, and if we
don't go now there won't be time before dinner.'

'Treasures to find?'

'Yes, to show Daddy. . .and Kylie. Special things
belonging to the desert, like—um—magic pebbles
and——'

Fortunately, since Susan's powers of inventiveness
were refusing to rise to the occasion, Simon had heard
enough. On the way out they encountered neither
Drew nor Kylie, but she heard their voices in the
kitchen. Drew was on the phone.

'Thanks, Jane,' he was saying. 'Yes, half an hour
would be good. With the time-difference, it's already
Simon's bedtime by Melbourne reckoning, and he had
an early start.'

Kylie was exclaiming loudly to no one in particular,

'I've *got* to have a cup of tea or I'll die! And then I've *got* to unpack. I can't *stand* living out of suitcases.'

It was wonderfully cool and fresh in the riverbed. Simon was eager to touch everything—the rounded pebbles, the hard, smooth trunks of the trees, the gritty sand that lay deep in some parts and that was quite wet below its dry surface. They did find some treasures too. Three perfect pale pink feathers from Major Mitchell cockatoos, a bluish pebble that 'might be a gemstone', Simon decided, and a special stick. Special to the little boy, anyway. Susan couldn't quite see why it was different from hundreds of other sticks, but she was happy to go along with Simon's opinion.

Twenty minutes passed very quickly and pleasantly, but then she had to say with reluctance, 'We'd better go back, Simon. It's dinnertime.' She had guessed from the snatch of phone conversation she had overheard that Jane Arnold would be bringing the promised casserole over at any moment, but for once she wasn't going to arrive back indoors with fifteen minutes to spare.

'I'm just going to find one more special gemstone for Daddy,' Simon said, and Susan felt no desire to rock his tentative happiness this evening by hurrying him along.

'There you are!' came a voice several minutes later. It was Drew, his footsteps grinding the river pebbles together with an almost musical note.

'Sorry. . .' Years of habit reasserted themselves and she felt quite contrite and agitated. 'Are we late?'

'A touch.'

'Oh, dear!'

'It doesn't matter, but we should get back before Jane's wonderful casserole gets cold.' He came up to her, rocking on a loose stone then steadying himself again, so that for a brief moment he was very close and she felt the warm fan of his breath. He glanced at Simon, who was some metres off and hadn't yet noticed

his father's arrival. 'You shouldn't have been saddled
with this,' he told Susan in a low voice.

'With what?' she asked, tilting up her chin, although
she knew what he meant.

'With Simon. It's Kylie's job.'

'It wasn't a problem, Dr Kershaw,' she told him very
deliberately. 'I wanted to explore and to get some fresh
air, and I could see that Simon needed distracting. He
was feeling a little blue when we first arrived.'

'Yes, well, Kylie should have seen that.'

You should have seen it, she wanted to tell him. She
didn't, though, remembering the scene they had had
last week in the café in Melbourne when he had asked
her not to comment on his relationship with the boy.
And she had promised she wouldn't—a promise that
she already knew would be hard to keep. . .

Perhaps comments were unnecessary, though. His
green-eyed gaze burned into her face as if he under-
stood exactly what she had been thinking, and for a
moment they were both frozen like this, their mutual
hostility quite apparent.

Drew's gaze was the first to falter, but that didn't
make Susan feel as if victory was hers. Instead she
suddenly felt drained and weak, too aware of the
doctor's almost threatening masculinity, and sharing
Simon's homesickness, as if she too were just a child.

Drew was calling to the boy now. 'What have you
found, Simon?'

'Oh, lots of things, Daddy. Look!'

He came hurrying over, across the treacherous surface of river pebbles, and all at once he had fallen,
bumping knees and forehead sharply on stone. Susan
gasped and lunged forward but Drew was quicker.
With a strangled exclamation he had reached the boy
and caught him up into his arms before the first cries
had even escaped from Simon's lips.

Cries? When they came, they were howls, so loud
and indignant that Susan relaxed. He wasn't badly

hurt, then. Silence would have been a more dangerous sign. To her surprise, though, Drew was still crushing the boy close and kissing the top of his head in between muttering soothing and rather incoherent phrases. There *was* blood coming from one knee and a red bruise already swelling on the child's temple, but really it was the kind of fall that an active child took in his stride every few weeks, and sometimes more often.

Why was Drew's reaction so strong?

'I want. . .to ring. . .Aunty Kate,' the child said jerkily as his sobs subsided.

'Of course. Of course. We'll do it right now,' Drew soothed, his voice almost as shaky as his son's. 'We should have done it as soon as we arrived. I wasn't thinking. I'm. . . I'm sorry, Simon.'

He carried the boy up to the house and went straight to the brand-new phone in the living-room, still holding him on his hip as he dialled the number from memory. Jane Arnold came out from the kitchen to see what was wrong. She held a handful of cutlery, which Susan took from her as she explained, 'He fell. Nothing to worry about.' Jane returned to the box of food she was unpacking and Susan began to set the dining-table as Drew spoke into the phone.

'Kate. . . ? Yes, we had a good trip. Simon wants to talk to you. He had a fall. . . No, he's fine. Just. . . well, homesick, of course. Here he is now.'

Drew handed the phone over and watched every expression on the little boy's face as he talked to his Aunty Kate. There was a hunger in those green eyes— Susan could see it clearly, even from across the room— and a watchfulness that contained jealously, bitterness, half a dozen emotions all mixed impossibly together.

He does love Simon, she realised. He loves him intensely. . .and painfully, when it should be such a simple thing. What on earth is going on with the man?

* * *

'Sorry, did I wake you up?' Kylie Radbone said cheerfully to Susan the next morning as the latter scraped sleep-tangled hair from her eyes, blinked and sat up on one elbow

'No, I was waking up on my own. What's the time?'

'Only about seven. Go back to sleep if you like. Dr Kershaw isn't up yet. Simon woke up at half-past five.'

'I didn't hear him. . .'

'Not your job. Nannies are trained to be early risers. At my last place, the baby used to be up by five every morning. Bit of a brat, it was. That's partly why I left.'

She rummaged in one of the drawers she had commandeered last night, found a cotton sweatshirt and dived into it. 'We've had breakfast and we're going outside. There's still a chill and some dew, but it's going to be gorgeous later on. See you. . .'

She thumped energetically out of the room in her black leather athletic shoes, leaving Susan with the impression that a colourful whirlwind had just passed through. The young nanny seemed to switch herself on and off like an electrical appliance. Last night, after calmly having her cup of tea and doing her unpacking as if no one else had any claim on her time at all, Kylie had suddenly devoted herself completely to the task of getting Simon fed, bathed, pyjamaed, read to and tucked into bed. What was more, she did a very good job of it, and Susan had seen both the little boy and his father grow much more relaxed.

'Time for his goodnight kiss, Dr Kershaw,' Kylie had said at precisely eight o'clock.

Relaxed? Drew Kershaw? Not any more. 'Goodnight kiss? Sure. . .' Gruffly spoken, reluctant. He had disappeared down the corridor, only to return less than a minute later with the relieved report, 'He's already asleep.'

Susan reached to the bedside table and looked at her watch. It was, as Kylie had said, just after seven and now she could hear Drew in the main bedroom across

the corridor opening and closing drawers as he dressed.
She did the same, choosing a neat cotton dress in
lemon and white. Uniforms, she hoped, would be at
the medical centre waiting for her.

They breakfasted together on toast, juice and coffee,
then argued politely over who would wash up—Kylie's
and Simon's dirty dishes were stacked on the sink as
well—until Susan took the mild initiative of suggesting
that they do it together.

It only took a few minutes, and neither spoke much,
but there was something alarmingly domestic about the
interlude. He washed while she rinsed and dried, and
several times their bare forearms nudged together.
Susan managed a flustered, 'Sorry!' each time until
Drew burst out impatiently.

'For heaven's sake, stop apologising every time you
touch me! I'm not made of glass.'

I am, though, Susan realised. I've worked with
dozens of male doctors and I've nursed men before,
seen quite a few of them stark naked, in fact. So why
did one brown forearm close to hers suddenly loom so
large in her awareness? She didn't know.

'Do you want more time to unpack?' Drew said
when they had finished.

'I don't want to unpack at all until I know where I'll
be staying,' she reminded him, and he nodded.

'Of course. Sorry. This must be unsettling for you.
I'll phone down to Perth and get it sorted out as soon
as their office opens.'

It was only just after eight when they unlocked the
door of the medical centre and began to gather their
first impressions of the place. Like Drew's house, it
was so new and had been so constantly shut up in the
several weeks since its completion that it smelled
overpoweringly of paint and other chemical fumes,
necessitating once again a wholesale throwing open of
windows. This time Drew joined in, and soon the place
felt fresher.

'I have the complete inventory here,' he said, putting a folder on to the reception desk. 'Everything from surgical gloves to waiting-room chairs. Uniforms for you, too, so you can dress even if you haven't got a house. Here.' He found the item on a list and quoted, 'Three, medium blue, size ten. Will that suit?'

'Sounds fine.'

'But don't bother to dig one out for today. We should go through this thing thoroughly, and that will probably take most of our time. And we should switch on the fridge. This afternoon the Flying Doctor Service is dropping off some supplies that need cold storage, including a complete set of snake anti-venoms.'

Susan couldn't help shuddering at his last words, and Drew saw it. 'Scared of them?'

She smiled ruefully at him. 'Aren't you?'

'I do hold them in healthy respect,' he admitted. 'The shy ones aren't a problem, I'm told. They hear you coming and make a dash for it. But there are a couple of more aggressive species out here. Kate told me she'd given Simon a very careful talk on leaving interesting-looking holes and hollow logs strictly alone.'

Susan smiled. 'I think I'll follow that advice as well.'

'Do. Kate grew up on a farm in the north-west of Victoria and knows what she's talking about.' He turned to the phone in the reception area. 'I'll try Perth now and see if we can get some answers on your accommodation problem.'

As he dialled, Susan thought about their snake discussion and realised that it was the first time he had mentioned Simon in a natural, relaxed way. She felt more relaxed as well. It was the desert, she decided, the air so clean and dry and fresh. Perhaps she wasn't going to detest Drew Kershaw quite as much as she had thought. . .

She sat in one of the very practical plastic waiting-room chairs and listened to him on the phone, noting

the way his manner changed through the ups and downs
of several phone calls. Mostly he was very professional
and very polite, his face serious, emphasising that
straight nose, and his voice crisp and pleasant on the
ear.

'I'm ringing from Coolacoola Medical Centre. Is
Colin Gates available?'

Occasionally, there was an impatient edge: 'All I
need to know is whether the department will pay for
Miss Carstairs' motel accommodation until her house
is ready!'

Finally came an outback friendliness that he was
clearly still cautious about. 'Mrs Shipton? I'm Drew
Kershaw, the new doctor here at Coolacoola. . .'

'I get the impression. . .' Susan began hesitantly as
he put down the phone at last.

'Yes,' he nodded, spreading his hands regretfully.
'It's maddening, and I'm truly sorry. If I'd had any idea
in Melbourne that this hadn't been sorted out. . . As
you might have gathered, I finally got the OK from the
health department to cover your motel bill for as long
as necessary, but now it seems that the motel can't put
aside a room for you. Not consistently, anyway. This
week is fine, but then they're booked up with a bus
tour next week. After that, a couple of weeks when
you could choose between three rooms most nights,
then come the school holidays and they're full again
for two weeks straight. Unless you'd prefer the camping ground. . .'

'Not really.'

'Then you might as well go on staying with me. With
us,' he amended quickly, and that familiar frown
returned, darkening his forehead and narrowing his
green eyes.

'I can easily take a caravan. . .' She responded to his
changed mood quickly.

'Don't be silly!' The dismissal was clearly meant to

be taken seriously. There was a short silence, then he added, 'Do you want to go and unpack now, then?'

'I can wait till tonight.'

He seemed relieved, and picked up the folder containing the inventory lists. Susan too was eager to get down to work after the morning's initial frustration. At noon they broke for lunch, and found Simon and Kylie making sandwiches in the kitchen. The little boy flung himself at Drew. 'I didn't see you this morning, Daddy,' he accused. 'You weren't awake.'

Drew was holding back again today, Susan saw. What on earth was eating him? That stiff hug, that unsmiling response. Now she doubted the love she had seen in him last night in the riverbed when Simon had fallen. He listened with far too little enthusiasm to their account of the morning.

'There are other kids here!' Simon told him, and Kylie filled in.

'Yes, we've met practically everyone. Bought a chocolate snack from Mrs Shipton at the motel. The Shiptons are quite young, and have twin girls aged three. Popped in on Jane Arnold—remember, she told us last night that we should—and met her little boys, who are two and four.'

'*I'm* four too,' Simon chipped in happily.

'And apparently the deputy ranger and his wife have a new baby, but I haven't met them yet. Matt and Margaret Latham.'

'That will make your job a little easier, then, won't it, Kylie?' was all Drew said. 'Entertainment for Simon. People for you to talk to.'

'I'm going to the Arnolds' this afternoon to ride Jeremy's bike,' Simon said, and this time it was Susan who had to respond.

'And you're getting your toys sent up here by freight, aren't you? Soon you'll have your own bike to ride, too!'

Half an hour later, she and Drew were back at work

on their inventory again. At three came an interruption when they drove out to the airport to meet the Royal Flying Doctor Service plane with its load of supplies. The medical centre was equipped with two four-wheel-drive vehicles for just such trips as this, as well as clinic or emergency visits to the iron ore mines and to several sprawling cattle stations, their homesteads almost like villages, that were within a hundred kilometres of here.

'We'll both get some practice with this thing, shall we?' Drew suggested as they climbed into the slightly larger vehicle of the two. 'I'll drive there and you drive back.'

The errand took quite a while. Drew practised putting the vehicle in and out of its lowest four-wheel-drive gears, and out at the airstrip they talked for fifteen minutes with the Flying Doctor Service's Dr Max Greeley and Sister Rose Portland. The new medical centre would have quite a bit of contact with the service, especially in the event of an emergency.

'But you're taking away some of our favourite clinic stops,' Rose Portland said. 'They always give us a wonderful lunch at Namburra Downs, and the mining camp has an indoor pool.' She grinned, an expression that softened her very square-cut face, and ran a hand through dark hair that looked dusty after her long day and that was far too bluntly cut to flatter the shape of her head. Definitely not a pretty woman, but she seemed pleasant.

'What was your background in Melbourne, Drew?' Max Greeley wanted to know, and the four of them argued in a casual, friendly way about whether emergency medicine in a big city hospital bore any relation to running a tiny clinic out in the desert.

Drew claimed that it did, and Susan was inclined to agree. Human beings were the same everywhere, underneath, and doctors and nurses had to think on their feet in any professional situation. But Max and Rose, both two-year veterans of the service, weren't prepared to concede that outback medicine had any similarity to anything else at all.

'They seem nice,' Susan commented as she took the wheel to drive back to the medical centre.

'Yes,' Drew agreed. 'And there's a potential friend for you in Rose.'

'When she lives so far away?' The Flying Doctor base was in Pendleton, a distance of over five hundred kilometres by road.

'Out here, I doubt that's important. It's more a question of having something in common. Coolacoola seems to be dominated by married couples with young children. You and Rose are both single. Ouch!'

Susan had pitched the left wheels of the vehicle straight into a deep, hard-edged pothole that had been largely concealed by the puddle of red dust it contained. There was a painfully loud bump, they lurched sideways, then she regained control and slowed down, a little shaken by the jerking and the noise, and knowing that she hadn't been concentrating on the road as she should have been.

Drew's casual comment had consigned her to the category of spinster, and for some reason that hurt. He hadn't meant it unkindly. In fact, a brief sideways glance at him told her that he wasn't aware he had upset her at all. . . And 'upset' was too strong.

I'm not surprised, am I, to find that he sees me that way? I'm sure most people do. Perhaps I see *myself* that way. Like Rose. Plain and practical. Nice. But not very sexy, and not very likely to get married. . . There was no more time to mull over the subject, which was probably a good thing.

'That took longer than I thought,' Drew said as Susan parked the four-wheel drive in front of the medical centre. 'And I really want to get that inventory knocked over by a reasonable hour. Kylie can't be on duty with Simon twenty-four hours a day. For one thing, I'm not paying her enough!'

It was meant to be a joke, and Susan laughed on cue, but she could sense once again the ambivalence in Drew Kershaw. Inside the building, they made instant coffee and worked as they drank it, finishing their task at about five. At Drew's house, Simon and Kylie were sitting quietly reading stories.

'We've had a nice quiet two hours,' the cheerful nanny reported. 'Jeremy really tired him out.'

But Simon rediscovered his energy at once when he saw Drew, and when he heard that he and his father were to make spaghetti together for tea. . .

He's *good* at fatherhood! Susan realised, listening to them in the kitchen as she relaxed for ten minutes with a glass of iced juice before tackling her unpacking. Silly voices, made-up songs, cooking tasks given to Simon that were just right for his four-year-old talents. . . What *is* holding him back? she wondered.

CHAPTER THREE

'You'll soon get the hang of it,' Tom Arnold told the new doctor and nurse after a comprehensive lesson with the medical centre's two-way radio equipment first thing the next morning. 'And if you have any problems, just give us a ring. There you are, you see! The telephone! A few years ago, we didn't have that, and used the two-way radio for everything. But with these new satellites, a lot of places have the phone on now and we don't use the radio nearly as much as we used to.'

'I'm bound to forget to use the proper call-signs and that sort of thing,' Susan said.

'No, you're not, because Matt Latham typed it all out for you yesterday. Pretty heroic, since he only uses two fingers.' The head ranger flourished a neat sheet of paper that had already been placed in a clear plastic sleeve.

'We'll tape it to the desk next to the equipment,' Drew said.

'Isn't it wonderful how friendly everyone is out here?' Susan said just after the ranger had gone. 'Sometimes in the city you feel you could fall through a crack in the floor and no one would notice, don't you? But here. . .'

'No, I've never felt that,' Drew answered absently. 'Look, could you dash after Tom and get him back before he drives off? According to this sheet he left, there's an open call-in session on the radio network between nine and nine-thirty every morning, and it's just after nine now. Seems as good a way as any to advertise that we're open for business now. We'll get Tom to oversee our first attempt at using this stuff.'

44

'Good idea,' she managed, and did as he had asked, catching up to the park ranger just as he pulled out on to Coolacoola's 'main street'.

He came back inside very willingly. Drew was already seated in front of the equipment, giving the medical centre's new call-sign and waiting to have it acknowledged. He looked confident and assured, and Susan doubted that Tom Arnold's help would be necessary at all. Of course Dr Drew Kershaw had never feared falling through a crack in the floor! And how silly to have confided to him her own too frequent sense of insignificance!

She felt herself grow hot as she watched him at the radio, and then was so distracted by her thoughts that when he motioned her to come and introduce herself over the airwaves she managed only a few flustered words and a complete muck-up of the signing-off procedure, simple enough though it was.

It was a relief when Tom Arnold left again and they could forget about the radio for the time being. Half an hour later, Drew told Lee Shipton, 'You have the honour of being our first patient.'

'Not me. It's the girls,' said the tall, sandy-blonde mother, who looked to be in her early thirties.

She had the three-year-old twins, Stacey and Corey, with her, and they looked adorable dressed in their practical cotton overalls—little blonde creatures with soft, peach-smooth skin. Peach-smooth in parts. This was what Mrs Shipton had come about.

'They've always had very tender, sensitive skin,' she said, 'and in the six months we've been at Coolacoola it's got much worse. Look at these rough red patches, and the way the slightest scratch gets so red around the edges, even when they've just scratched themselves with their fingernails, or rubbed at any itchy mosquito bite.'

Susan thought she knew what Drew would do—take a brief look, suggest insect-repellent to keep mosquitoes at bay and prescribe a mild cortisone cream for what was obviously some kind of eczema. He didn't, though. Instead, he spent nearly half an hour with Mrs Shipton and the girls, and when they emerged from his surgery the mother had a long list of suggestions for care written out by Dr Kershaw on the medical centre's new stationery. She had instructions to come back next week too, as well as the expected prescription.

Susan got the cream from the dispensary and dealt with the paperwork, then said when the girls and their mother had gone, 'It wasn't just eczema, then?'

'Oh, it was eczema all right, but there was no sense in simply prescribing the cream. The water out here is as hard as nails, insect bites are unavoidable, and there's a lot of dust and dirt in even the daintiest three-year-old's life.'

'No outback child can be dainty!'

'Exactly. And diet could be a factor as well. I suggested all sorts of things—oatmeal baths, pure cotton clothing, filtered water, extra care in keeping fingernails short and clean so that when they scratch themselves it doesn't get inflamed.'

'You're very thorough, aren't you?'

'I've got a chance to be, at last, I hope. I like to get to the bottom of things, not just settle for superficial solutions. But in Melbourne our casualty department was always so busy I never had time. Hell, it's good!'

He sat back in his swivel chair, locking his fingers behind his head as he gave a relaxed, satisfied grin. Susan couldn't help grinning back, then suddenly she found she was blushing, and didn't have the slightest idea why.

'Would you like a cup of coffee and a biscuit?' she asked him quickly. 'It's halfway through the morning already, and——'

'Sounds good. . .'

* * *

'Dr Kershaw! Drew!' The urgent voice interrupted the sleepiest time of the afternoon, three o'clock, when there was no patient at the new centre and consequently little to do. Three men from the mining camp had turned up just after lunch with minor ailments, but they were long gone.

'We'll work out a timetable for routine appointment hours and an on-call roster that divides the load between us,' Drew had been saying. 'No sense in us both——'

It was Jane Arnold's voice that had cut off his words. She clattered up the steps and burst through the door seconds later, and both Drew and Susan were at once on their feet. The tall, pretty park ranger's wife was panting and red-faced, and beside her she almost dragged Simon, who was sobbing breathlessly and quite distraught.

'What is it?' Drew barked.

'Snake-bite——'

'My God!' He turned pale, looked at Simon, and clutched the front desk for support.

'Not Simon,' Jane Arnold almost shouted. 'Kylie. From Simon's description it was a King Brown, so there's no time to lose.'

'Where is she?'

'Still where it happened, on the rocky outcrop up behind our place. She panicked totally, I think, but Simon ran all the way down by himself to find help, the brave little thing.'

'Thank God we got the anti-venoms yesterday!'

'She tried to kill it with a stick and it bit her,' Simon sobbed. 'It kept biting her.'

'I should have told them not to go up there. I knew Tom had seen a King Brown in those rocks recently, but——'

'Can we drive?' Drew interrupted urgently. At this stage, any self-recrimination only wasted precious time.

'Yes, most of the way. It's rough, *very* rough, but——'

'We can't have her walking down. The more she moves, the quicker she pumps that venom through her system. Perhaps Tom——'

'Tom and Matt are both on the far side of the park all day.'

'Then I'll have to.' Without wasting any more time, he took the medical centre's four-wheel-drive keys from a box under the desk and almost snatched at the snake indentification kit that Susan had given him. 'Simon——' he squatted to bring himself level with the frightened little boy, and his voice almost choked over the name '——you were very brave to get help so quickly. Now you have to stay and help Susan.'

He put out a shaking hand and touched the fair hair gently, muttered, 'Thank God it wasn't you. . .' and then was standing again, already striding to the door. The square set of his shoulders showed that the moment of broken emotion was already behind him.

Moments later the vehicle had roared away down the street, with Jane Arnold in the passenger seat.

'I'm brave,' the little boy said to Susan, still sobbing intermittently.

'I know you are, and brave boys need a chocolate biscuit and a glass of milk, don't they?'

'Yes.'

'Your daddy and I have some special injections to give Kylie that will stop the snake-bite from poisoning her and soon she'll be better again. Isn't that clever?'

'Yes.' Gradually the frightened sobs subsided, and then there was silence as Simon drank his milk and Susan made preparations for Kylie's treatment.

As soon as she had a spare moment, she opened the back door of the building and could see the four-wheel drive in the distance, making a cloud of dust as it lurched and ground its way up the rough, rocky slope behind the Arnolds' house. She could hear the sounds it made—vicious bangs as metal chassis met rock, inhuman groans and grindings from the protesting engine. Beyond, she could see a tiny, colourful shape that must be Kylie, though from this distance she couldn't tell whether the girl was sitting or standing. . . or even alive. No, surely they would get to her in time! Even the worst envenomation took several hours to bring death.

The Commonwealth Serum Laboratories provided venom-detection and snake-identification kits, and this morning, after Mrs Shipton's departure, Drew and Susan had both read up on the treatment of venomous bites from creatures in this region. Neither had expected to need the materials nor the information so soon. In spite of the Australian bush's reputation for venomous creatures, snake- and spider-bites really weren't an everyday occurrence.

Susan found now that some of what she had read this morning was gone from her head in the drama of the moment. How confident was Drew? And Jane? She was a city woman, originally from Perth, and had been living in the outback, here and further north, since her marriage six years ago. How often had she encountered the reality of a King Brown bite?

The vehicle had stopped now, still some fifty yards from where Kylie was. Evidently Drew just couldn't negotiate the rough terrain any further. Now it was impossible to see what was happening. Two human shapes had joined that colourful blob just below the big, sculpted cubes of rust-red rock. Susan blinked and squeezed her eyes. The light was so bright, shimmering and glaring over the landscape. It was pointless to keep watching.

Behind her, she heard Simon overflow into tears once again and realised that she couldn't neglect the little boy. She had already prepared the equipment necessary for inserting an intravenous line, as well as locating the drugs that would be needed. The anti-venom would be diluted with normal saline, oxygen would probably be given, and Kylie would be pre-medicated with adrenaline and antihistamine to guard against the severe allergic reaction known as anaphy-laxis, that could occur with the use of antivenom. There was nothing more she could do for the nanny now. Better devote her full attention to someone she *could* help. . .

'I ran down and got Jane and Daddy,' Simon said for perhaps the fifth time.

Several minutes had passed since Susan had stopped looking out of the back door, and the child, though calm again now, still clearly needed reassurance and explanations repeated over and over as he tried to make sense of what had happened.

'You did just the right thing,' Susan told him.

Then she heard the sound of the vehicle outside. Drew carried Kylie in, her punctured forearm immo-bilised with a pressure bandage, and the first warning symptoms of nausea, sweating and headache beginning to appear. 'I'm going to give the adrenaline subcutan-eously,' Drew said. 'Point three mils of one in a thousand solution. And promethazine HC1 too. We'll take some blood for positive identification first, although everything points to a King Brown, and we'll use the eighteen thousand units of Black Snake anti-venom that's recommended.'

'Diluted?'

'Yes, ten times, and we'll try to get it in over twenty minutes. Dangerous to do it too fast. . .'

There was a lot to do, and the line between the danger of the venom itself and the body's reaction to the anti-venom could be a fine one. Kylie would need close monitoring for twenty-four hours as it had been known for a snake-bite victim to be discharged in apparent good health after treatment, only to be admit-ted acutely ill hours later. Nursing care would be similar to that of a head injury, with Kylie being examined hourly.

'How long since you had a tetanus shot?' Susan asked the young nanny as soon as the more urgent treatments had been given.

'I can't remember. . .' Her reactions were still fuzzy and slow, she had already vomited twice and had complained that her headache was severe. Her blood-pressure was alarmingly low as well, increasing her feeling of faintness and disorientation. 'Oh, yes!' she said at last. 'A few years ago, just after I finished my training course. . .'

So that was one treatment that could be crossed off the list, but Drew prescribed an antibiotic, as the skin around the scattering of puncture marks on Kylie's arm had been dusty with outback dirt. Eventually, as darkness fell, there was nothing further to do but monitor the young woman's condition, and Drew and Susan were able to assess what had happened and begin to write up notes on the case in some detail.

They sat in Drew's office to do this, and when the doctor looked up from his writing it was to say with quiet, thoughtful satisfaction, 'I think we did well over this, don't you?'

'Are you surprised?' she answered him.

'Well, it was a new experience for both of us, and that isn't always easy. I know even in Casualty, where I was constantly presented with new variations on old medical themes, there was the danger of working from habit, forgetting how to take initiative, or panicking at the idea of a new treatment.'

'Panicking? Losing initiative? That sounds very much out of character for you, Drew,' she told him mildly, a little surprised at herself for daring to give this frank analysis.

Would he be angry? No. He laughed. 'Perhaps, but we're all a little afraid of that sometimes, don't you think? Ruining our careers by just one small moment of acting out of character?'

'Or one very large moment of acting *in* character, in some cases.'

'In your case? Nonsense! You're not the panicking type!' It was spoken with flattering confidence. In fact, both of them had spoken with confidence about aspects of each other's personality that they seemed to know surprisingly well after such a short acquaintance. It was interesting. . .unsettling. . .satisfying.

Drew closed his folder of notes and stood up, preparing to leave. Simon had gone home with Jane Arnold for the evening meal, and it was time to collect him now. Tinned soup had formed a simple but adequate tea for Drew and Susan. Kylie had not been given anything to eat, as oral intake of food and liquid might still prove dangerous, but she was resting peacefully now, and there were no signs of anaphylaxis or of further envenomation.

'Looks as if that initial eighteen thousand units will be enough,' Drew said, 'but we still can't be sure. We'll continue the hourly observations. Meanwhile, when you get tired, curl up on that second ward bed and take an hour's sleep. Better set the alarm. . .'

'It's in the store-room, isn't it?'

'Yes.' Seconds later, he was on his way to pick up Simon from the Arnolds' house, and for four hours the medical centre was very quiet. . .

At just after midnight, Susan completed another hourly noting of blood-pressure, pulse, temperature, respiration and other signs, and knew that she really ought to take Drew's advice about getting some rest. Somehow, though, she didn't yet feel sleepy. It was nice just to sit here in the comfortable chair in Drew's office reading about far-away places in a very light paperback novel. She had just finished chapter two when she heard footsteps on the veranda and a moment later Drew had entered.

'You didn't have to come,' she told him. 'I would have called you if anything didn't look good.' Kylie's blood-pressure had improved and she no longer complained of any pain or nausea. There were none of the signs of more serious systemic envenomation. No muscle paralysis or weakness, no drooping eyelids, double vision or swallowing difficulty. 'So go and get some sleep,' she finished.

He looked vulnerable tonight, his face pale so that the freckled bridge of his nose stood out. Perhaps it was hardly surprising after what had happened.

'I tried to sleep earlier,' he admitted. 'I couldn't. This is a horrible mess, isn't it? A horrible start here for Simon, to lose his new nanny, and so dramatically, after just two days.'

Susan blurted, surprised, 'You don't think she's still in danger?'

'No, no, she's going to be fine, but. . . I can't see how I can keep her on.' He paced the room unseeingly, picked up a glass paperweight and put it down again. 'Her behaviour with that snake was idiotic. She told us about it when we first got to her, and from what I can gather the creature wasn't a threat to her or to Simon at all until she went at it with a stick.'

'Norah in the *Billabong* books I used to read as a child did that quite often, it seemed,' Susan came in gently. 'Thwacked them a good hard thwack on the spine. It always worked for her. They expired immediately with a wriggle or two.'

Drew smiled unwillingly. 'Yes, Australian literature and lore is full of that sort of thing, isn't it? But the thinking on that has changed now. We don't use tourniquets, we don't incise the wound, and we *don't* try to kill the creatures. For one thing, so many species are protected. For another, it's crazy to try to kill a snake if you don't know how to do it well. Much better to leave it alone and back off calmly. All Kylie must have done was madden the creature with her flailing blows. She says she tried to hit it at least half a dozen times, but only made contact twice. Its aim, on the other hand, was a lot more accurate!'

'Simon is afraid it was hurt.'

'Is he. . .? There was no sign of the creature when we got there. I must tell him not to worry about it.' He turned to face Susan and pulled the swivel chair from behind his desk around so that he could sit closer to her. 'Susan, I don't know what to do. I like Kylie well enough. Simon seems to like her, and yet. . .'

'She's competent in what she does,' Susan said slowly, trying not to show how surprised she was that he seemed to be confiding in her. His face was creased in thought and he was hunched forward in the chair, elbows resting on hard knees and shoulders held tightly.

'But she's got no initiative,' he was saying. 'She's still carrying round her notes from nanny school, I discovered last night. Or when she does use some initiative, like today, it seems foolish and poorly thought-out. Am I over-reacting to feel that I can't entrust my——' He stopped and drew a breath, then went on in a slightly altered tone, 'Can't entrust Simon to someone who is going to panic in the bush? What if they got lost? What if Simon fell and broke a bone? Am I being unjust?'

'Does it really matter, Drew, whether you are or you aren't?' she asked him gently. 'This isn't like having a secretary who told you she could type a hundred words a minute and then you discover she can only do fifty-five. You're Simon's father. You have to trust the person who looks after him every day, and you don't have to justify your trust or mistrust with a list of facts. She's owed some pay in lieu of notice, and her fare to Melbourne, and that's all.'

'Simon's father. . .' Drew murmured, then he got to his feet and began pacing again. 'Perhaps I *am* letting reasonless emotion dictate to me tonight. I can't dis-

miss Kylie on such grounds. Simon can't afford to have
me turn into some over-protective. . .'

He stopped and punched a fist into the palm of his
other hand, then went on decisively, 'I'll keep her. I
have to keep her, for Simon's sake and mine.'

'If that's what you think is right. . .'

'It is. And if she blows this second chance I'll give
her the proper month's notice.'

'That's certainly fair.' Susan frowned, confused at
his rapid change of tack. He had taken the opposite
guidance from her tentative advice to what she had
intended, and the decision he had made didn't seem to
have relaxed him.

'There's condensed milk and chocolate powder
here,' she offered after a moment. 'I could make us
some hot chocolate before you go back to bed.'

'Hmm?' He looked across at her out of the distant
landscape of his thoughts. 'Hot chocolate? Yes, that'd
be nice.'

She went away without saying anything more and
busied herself at the small stove and fridge, returning
five minutes later with the steaming drinks in two thick
mugs. Drew wasn't there. She was standing in the
middle of his office just beginning to get a little angry
and confused when he returned.

'I went to check on Simon,' he explained at once. 'I
thought he might have a bad night after today's events,
but so far he's been sleeping peacefully. He's always
been a good sleeper, actually. Slept through the night
at five weeks. I remember when Lisa——' He stopped
abruptly, a reminiscent smile draining rapidly from his
face.

There was a pause, then Susan came in carefully,
'Here's your hot chocolate, Drew.'

'Thanks.'

He took it from her, inwardly cursing the sweep of
contradictory and sometimes not very admirable
emotions he had been forced to experience today.

Anger against Kylie, that painful, bitter love for Simon, and the impotent fury he still felt against his dead wife which threatened so often to spill into what he felt for every other human being in his life as well.

'Is anything the matter, Drew?'

He looked at her. Only the reading-lamp on his desk had been switched on to illuminate her book, which she had now closed and put aside. In the yellowish, angled light, her medium-brown hair took on golden highlights and her profile was etched in shadow and brightness. Her dark brown eyes, studying him so seriously and with a concern that he had to be flattered by, were large, swimming pools and her neat mouth was as straight as a pin. She really had rather a sweet face. . .

'Nothing's the matter,' he told her unwillingly, and untruthfully.

She took a deep breath and went on, 'It must have been very hard for you, your wife's death.' Her empathy was palpable, and suddenly he couldn't stand having yet another person in his life who tiptoed around the issue of his widowhood and avoided the name 'Lisa' as if he would shatter at the sound of it.

He had come here to Coolacoola to make a fresh start of sorts, hadn't he? And he would be spending large chunks of every day with this spinsterish little creature who had already revealed surprising depths of perception and some uncomfortably strong opinions. Why not try honesty for a change? Susan Carstairs would be his guinea-pig in the experiment.

'Lisa's death hard?' he echoed, just when he knew she had decided that he wasn't going to respond at all. 'Yes, it was hard. Death is always hard when it cuts short a process that needs to be completed.'

'I don't——'

'No, you don't understand,' he agreed, before the sentence was halfway out of that serious mouth. 'I'm talking about divorce. My marriage to Lisa was miserable almost from the beginning. She never should have married a doctor. . .and I never should have married a model. That was only part of it, of course. Unfortunately, she decided more quickly than I did that our fights and misunderstandings weren't just symptoms of the adjustments that every couple has to make to married life. I was such a fool!'

'You persevered,' Susan said, frowning as she took in the weight of every word with her brown eyes still fixed on him. 'I can't see that that's so foolish, or reprehensible.'

'Really? You don't think that I was a fool not to suspect that she was simply staying with me until a better prospect came along? And when he did—Craig Osborne was his name—she left. . .although I should mention that there was a joyous little period when, unbeknown to me, she was sleeping with both of us!'

'Oh!' He had shocked her, he saw at once, and he felt bad about it. Clearly, she had seen little of life, but it was too late now to have this sudden urge to protect her innocence. He had no choice but to go on. 'I didn't suspect, in fact, until the night she left me to go with Craig, and three days after that they were both killed in an accident. It saved me from the hassle of divorce, didn't it?' He laughed, letting the bitterness into it.

'Well, yes, but. . .' she whispered.

'But?'

'But it took away your chance to forgive.'

Very simple words, but they were just right, and put a huge parcel of his feelings into a clear perspective which three years of angry introspection had never given him.

'You're a bit of a witch, aren't you?' he whispered.

'What? A witch?' She was startled and her eyes widened.

'Yes, you see you're right. I still haven't forgiven Lisa, because she isn't here to forgive. My God!'

He felt emotion catch in his throat and got quickly

to his feet, never having expected this talk with his nurse tonight to leave him so vulnerable. He heard Kylie groan in her sleep in the small hospital room next door, and Susan pricked up her ears at the sound as well, but then there was silence again.

She said very carefully, 'I've wanted to know since last week why your feelings about Simon are so. . . complicated,' was the word she finally chose. 'And now I *do* know, don't I? He's part of Lisa, and with him in your life you can't forget.'

'Forget? Never! And. . .' Tumbling words leapt to his lips and then died. He couldn't tell her the full complexity of it all. He just couldn't. 'I couldn't forget. That's right,' he sighed.

The drinking chocolate was getting cold. He took several gulps, moved to the doorway, and felt the mood of confession slipping from him. Susan sat there sipping her own drink and saying nothing. She was a wise little thing and must know that the last thing he wanted was to hear an extended commentary on what he had confided. Perhaps it was nursing that had given her this wisdom, and yet he had known some pretty foolish and insensitive nurses in his time.

Then he remembered what she had told him about her childhood—feeling guilty, of course, because he hadn't listened properly to half of it. Perhaps it was that. Unhappy children were often wise beyond their years. . .

'I'd better get back to bed,' he said.

She stood up, with an automatic and rather old-fashioned politeness, and he knew that she was going to walk him to the door.

'Jane Arnold has offered to look after Simon again tomorrow,' he told her as she approached. 'So you can get some sleep and have the day to yourself, barring emergencies, once I relieve you here after breakfast.'

'I will be tired, I think,' she admitted in that voice that continued to surprise him with its understated contralto notes. Somehow, she looked like the type that would pipe or bleat or squeak. But then, he was quickly coming to realise that she wasn't a 'type' at all.

They met up in the doorway of the small, newly fitted-out surgery. She had continued to move forward, clearly expecting that he would lead the way along the corridor, but he hadn't. He was still standing there propped up against the door-frame, distracted by the pointless skittering of his thoughts. And as she stopped beside him, that chin tilted as she looked up with a tiny frown of confusion, he realised something.

My God, I want to kiss her!

That mouth really was so perfectly formed, the sensitivity mirrored in those chocolate-brown eyes was so very strong and warm. . . You could swim in it, swim in that mouth. . .

He came to his senses just in time. It would be disastrous if he kissed her. Totally disastrous! It didn't take much perception to guess that she had probably never been kissed before. Kissed properly, that was. He discounted schoolboy fumblings and the hit-or-miss approach of party-prone medical students. It wasn't misplaced arrogance which told him that any kiss he gave those innocent lips would be far more powerful and dangerous to her than anything she had experienced before. It was a fact. He was a man, experienced and mature, a seasoned thirty-four years old against her untried twenty-three.

With quite an effort, he managed to draw back. Had she guessed his intention? Her lips were parted now, and her pupils darkly dilated. A tiny breath sighed from her mouth and then the tip of a delicately pink tongue darted nervously across the full bow that arched over her upper teeth.

'Goodnight, Drew,' she said huskily. 'I'll. . . I'll lock up, I think. Probably a very city-bred thing to do, but. . .'

'Of course. If it makes you feel safer. I have the

keys, so you needn't even worry about being awake between hourly observations to let me in tomorrow morning.'

'Oh, I'll be awake,' she told him.

And then he had gone. Susan couldn't help watching him disappear into the outback darkness along the walkway that led to his house. She doubted now that she would sleep at all. He had almost kissed her. She was sure of it, and yet it seemed ridiculous even to think of the idea. A man like that. A girl. . .a woman like her.

Her heart was pounding so hard in her chest that it seemed to be hurting her throat, and she could almost taste his lips on hers as if they really had been there. The scent of him—frankly male, with a hint of pine-tinged aftershave, and disturbingly pleasant—seemed to linger in the air, so that she wanted to reach out and draw it to her, like drawing his body close. . .

No! For heaven's sake! She must have imagined the whole thing. A man eleven years her senior, who had been through a painful, failed marriage and fathered a child.

And me, a plain little spinsterish nurse. He'd laugh if he knew! I'm laughing myself. What a fantasy! After all, I don't even like him much. . .do I? she thought.

A treacherous well of sensation deep in her body insisted that this last issue didn't matter in the slightest.

CHAPTER FOUR

'I'M SORRY, Dr Kershaw, I can't stay on here,' Kylie
Radbone said two days later. 'You'll have to work out
some other arrangement for tomorrow.'

She made the announcement abruptly as they sat at
dinner, after Drew had asked her whether she felt fit
enough to resume full-time care of Simon the next
morning. He and Susan would be spending the entire
day out at the Jambarra mine, doing a regular check-
up on mine workers.

'What do you mean, "some other arrangement"?' he
hissed explosively. Simon looked startled and upset,
and Susan knew that his sensitive soul must have picked
up on the fact that his care was a complicating factor
for everyone.

'I mean I want to go back to Melbourne straight
away, as soon as there's a way to get out of here.'
Kylie's round blue eyes met his green ones quite
calmly. 'You do see, don't you, how impossible it
would be to stay? Ughh. . .!' She shivered. 'I'd be
terrified even to set foot outside the door. The snake
just *came* at me, and I nearly died!'

'If that's how you feel,' Drew growled. Susan could
see that he was keeping his control with difficulty.

'It *was* bad luck, Kylie,' she came in, trying to
appease both of them. 'But you know now how to——'

'Bad luck?' the bright blonde jeered

'—how to deal with snakes.'

'That is, leave them strictly alone,' Drew interjected
ominously.

'So in a few days I'm sure you'll relax again and——'

'No!' Kylie almost shouted. 'I'm *not* staying! OK?
Please, Dr Kershaw, I want you to phone around and

61

get me on a plane or a truck to Pendleton—anything!—
tomorrow!'

'I'm not hungry,' Simon said in his little voice at that
moment.

'Aren't you, love? Actually, I'm not very hungry
either,' Susan came in quickly. 'But hey! I know! It's
still warm outside and not dark yet. Maybe if we took
our dinner out on to the veranda in the fresh air, we'd
get an appetite. We'll have a picnic, shall we? And
we'll get some lemonade and some cake for dessert.'

He brightened at once and agreed to the idea, and
she was thankful that she had made hamburgers tonight
as well as a packet cake mix, since these things lent
themselves well to an improvisation that was only
designed to take the little boy out of earshot of this
scene between Drew and Kylie.

'Boy! We *were* hungry after all,' she was able to say
to him twenty minutes later as the last mouthfuls of
food disappeared and the last gulps of fizzy lemonade
were drained.

They had seated themselves on the steps below the
veranda and were watching the sunset parade of galahs
and other birds wheeling and screeching in the huge
leafy crowns of the river gums. Now footsteps came
behind them and Drew sat down too, touching a hand
to Simon's shoulder before saying quietly to Susan,
'Thanks for seeing what he needed then.'

'It wasn't hard. . .'

'No, you're very good at it. . . I just rang the mining
camp. They have a plane going to Pendleton first thing
tomorrow and they'll take her. We can drop her out
there. Jane is going to take Simon again tomorrow. . .'

'And after that?'

'I have no idea,' he told her heavily. 'And I can't
think about it now. It's Friday night. Even if some
agency in Perth could fly someone up, I can't organise
it till Monday.'

His tone told her clearly that he didn't want to talk

about it any more. As if to underline this, he said loudly and cheerfully to Simon, 'Want to walk up to the beginning of the gorge and see if we can find any kangaroos coming down to the waterhole for their evening drink?'

'Yes, please!'

'Let's get the torch, then, because we'll have to walk back in the dark.'

After they had gone, Susan went inside and cleared up the meal, while in the background came the sound of Kylie's thumping feet going to and fro as she emptied wardrobe and drawers and packed up her things.

The small plane gathered speed on the runway, gave a lurch and a hop, then was airborne, skimming over a few gnarled bushes before gaining height at a rapid rate and straining noisily for the endless arc of blue sky above. Jambarra Mine's airstrip was eerily silent now. Kylie had gone. For a moment neither Drew nor Susan spoke as they stood beside the medical centre's four-wheel drive, then, 'We have work to do,' Drew said.

The morning that followed came as a relief after the past few days of drama over Kylie's snake-bite and abrupt departure. Minex International liked to know that its workers were healthy, and organised annual check-ups for every employee. Formerly, these had been done by the Royal Flying Doctor Service, but they were happy to surrender this extra load, and now it was the job of the new Coolacoola medical staff.

The check-ups were staggered at intervals throughout the year, depending on when each man had joined the company, and today Drew and Susan had to see twenty men, as well as four who had current medical complaints. This added up to a solid stream, and inevitably they ran late. It was already half an hour after the scheduled lunch-break when Ted Leighton arrived in the small mine office where Susan did routine blood-pressure and other checks before handing each patient over to Drew in a bigger office—today a makeshift surgery—next door.

The man immediately struck her as unappealing, but she tried to get over this prejudice. A red face, bulbous nose, leering smile and hefty beer gut didn't *necessarily* mean that he was awful. She returned his smile and began her work. Reflexes, chest and heart sounds, blood-pressure, pulse-rate. . .

'This is nice, darling,' he commented with a chuckle and a drawl after several minutes, 'but I'm not on your routine check-up list.'

'You're not?' Flustered at his over-familiar manner, she glanced down at the typed sheet of patient names. She hadn't bothered to check it when he came in, as, after the extra-early start this morning, she was ready for lunch now and was happy that this man was the last patient of the morning session.

'Nope, I'm not,' he grinned.

'You should have said so,' she told him shortly, although in general she hated to be rude to patients.

This man, though, obviously *wanted* to provoke her discomfort. He went on, 'No, the reason I'm here, love, is 'cos I've got a ——' He used a coarse euphemism that it took her several seconds to understand, and he watched, with that same offensive leer, her initial confusion and growing comprehension. 'Sorry, I've forgotten the proper name for it,' he drawled.

'Gonorrhoea,' she supplied with a snap. She had encountered it before.

'That's right. Don't know which of 'em I got it from. . .'

'Which what?'

'Oh, you know, love. Let's see, what can I call them so I don't make your ears go red? Professional girls. Ladies of the night. There was three of 'em, see, on my last leave in Pendleton. So I need your doc to give me some stuff for it, OK?'

'We'll have to do some tests to make sure it's——'

'I know what it is. Had it before, haven't I?'

'To make sure your friends didn't give you anything else as well,' she finished very firmly.

She could see that he wanted to shock her, and he had. Nursing had never been a career to go into if you were squeamish or overly puritanical. But there were limits, and she had reached them! She didn't want to hear any more of this man's gleeful anecdotes about what ailed him and how it had all come about. There were certain clinical facts that she had to record on his patient history chart, but that was all.

Unfortunately, he resisted all her attempts to keep their discussion to a professional level, insisting on providing her with details that she had no desire and no medical need to know, and by the time she was ready to hand him over to Dr Kershaw she was feeling quite sick. The man had been deliberately trying to get to her.

Tidying up the paperwork from this morning's long list of patients helped somewhat, but she was still churned up when Drew poked his head around her door at last and said, 'Ready to go and find this canteen lunch they've been promising us?'

'Very ready,' was all she could say.

If he noticed her state, he didn't comment on it.

They left the long, low prefabricated building that housed the mine's offices and crossed a dusty square of dirt, criss-crossed with enormous tyre-marks, to arrive at a larger building, also made of prefabricated sections, where the canteen was sending forth savoury smells. Most of the men had eaten already, it seemed, but there was plenty of food left—hearty, generous plates of stew and steak, chips, salad, bread, custard, cake, jelly. . .

Susan's appetite had gone.

'You should eat,' Drew told her absently as they slid their red plastic trays along the grooved metal bench. He looked tired and distant, and she guessed that he had slept badly last night, and was worrying about Simon again now as well.

'Just this salad will be fine.'

'Salad?' He looked critically at her plate. 'That's a lettuce leaf, a gherkin and a slice of cheese the size of a small Band-aid!'

'Really, I'm not. . .' she began, but he had seen her distress now.

'Hey. . .what's wrong?'

'That man. . .'

'Who? Oh, our last chap. Hmm. . .' He looked at her closely and her pallor was suddenly replaced by a flush. 'Yes, he wasn't very pleasant, was he?'

'He let me think at first that he was there for a check-up, then. . .'

'It's easily treatable, if he hasn't caught anything else with it.' He tossed off the reassurance, which wasn't what she was seeking, then his voice slowed and he eyed her even more narrowly. 'It really shocked you, didn't it?'

'Yes. . .' She supposed that 'shocked' was the word. Nauseated, really. Not his disease so much, although with all its connotations it was an unpleasant one, but the way he had enjoyed thrusting the whole sordid tale right under her nose.

'You haven't seen a lot of life, have you?'

'I suppose not.'

'Look, what can we do about this? We've got twelve more patients to see. That's another three hours at least, and then the drive back. I don't like the idea of you doing it on an empty stomach, and there's no guarantee that there won't be more men of Mr Leighton's ilk.'

'I'll be all right.'

'You obviously don't want a hot lunch, and neither do I. We've got forty minutes. Let's make ham and salad rolls for ourselves out of this lot and save them for later. You brought your swimming togs, didn't you?'

'Yes. . .'

'I was going to suggest a swim when we finished for the day, but I think you need one now.'

'That does sound much better,' she admitted.

Drew took control, not sorry that he had something else to think about. He needed that badly today, having spent—as his nurse probably suspected from his tired eyes—half the night lying awake wondering what to do about Simon. Could he possibly send the boy back to Melbourne? Kate and Charles could hire a nanny themselves, and he would cover the cost. . .

No. Out of the question. He didn't stop to ask himself why this was so, he just knew that it was.

Having such a steady stream of patients this morning—even men like Ted Leighton—had been a relief, and now that Miss Carstairs needed his masculine support because she had been sent into a maidenly tizzy by a mild case of gonorrhoea. . .

But no, it wasn't a maidenly tizzy. It was more than that. She really was revolted by the whole thing, and in spite of his assessment of her naïveté he was surprised at the depth of her response. She must have encountered venereal disease and other equally unpleasant things before this. Surely she must!

The evidence of her response, though, suggested that she hadn't, and he found, somewhat to his surprise, that he felt quite protective towards her because of it. Really, she was almost a child. . .

Five minutes later they had put on swimming costumes, gathered towels, and had arrived at the pool. It, too, was housed in a prefab building, and wasn't large but looked inviting all the same.

Her costume was awful, he saw as she dropped her towel and toed the water tentatively. Yellow was *not* the colour to flatter fair, freckled skin, although she was already beginning to tan a little in the desert sun.

The cut of the thing, too, was almost laughably modest. It was one of those racing suits, very plain and athletic, but without the clever cutting and shaping that the latest styles showed off so well. She must have had it for years.

He realised that her nurse's salary had not stretched much beyond the upkeep of her house and the payment of day-to-day expenses, but all the same the price of one new swimming costume. . .!

She had caught his unthinking stare and was flushing. He looked quickly away, but it was too late and he cursed himself for not hiding his attitude better. There was no need to hurt her. . .

'Admiring my suit?' she was saying, the bright tone not quite genuine. 'Charming, isn't it? The washing machine ate my good one last Saturday and there wasn't time to buy another before we came up.'

'No, must have been a bit of a rush,' he muttered, thoroughly ashamed of himself now. She was a brave creature—unexpectedly so—bringing the thing out into the open like that instead of nursing the hurt of his rudeness—a rudeness he now chastised himself for roundly.

Still uncomfortable, he threw his towel aside and plunged into the water, making his leap just long enough after hers to see that her dive was neat and extremely graceful, defying his expectations yet again.

'Thanks, Drew,' she said afterwards, when they had dressed and were munching their salad rolls in the sun outside the pool building.

'For what?' he answered her, watching the way a strand of her hair lifted itself silkily, in the light breeze, from the still wet mass beneath, and dried to reveal ginting golden-brown threads.

'For suggesting the swim and these rolls. I feel much better now. Perhaps I over-reacted before.'

'Well, if it was how you felt. . .' he excused her inanely.

Privately, he was forced to conclude that she *had* over-reacted, and hoped that they wouldn't encounter similar problems in the future. Some of the people out here in the Dymock Ranges—eccentrics, loners, bush people from way back—led unconventional lives. She couldn't afford, and neither could he, to let her personal morals affect her work.

'We'd better get back to it,' he told her a few minutes later as they finished eating.

It was after five when they set off again for Coolacoola. 'I told Jane I thought we'd be back by now,' Drew said to Susan with a frown as he took the wheel.

'She'll understand. Don't try and take this road too fast, please!' Susan told him lightly.

Special trains brought the iron ore from the mine to the railhead on the coast, but large trucks often thundered up and down the unsealed road, creating deep corrugations and potholes as they brought in supplies, including building materials. Definitely not a road for high-speed driving.

As they swung out of the mining camp, Susan saw the almost completed new recreation building standing next to the long prefab quarters where the men were housed. There was no building crew visible at the moment, but of course it was late on a Saturday afternoon. She wished they would get on with the job and get back to working on her own house!

This wish strengthened almost into a prayer that night when she and Drew arrived back at Coolacoola. Simon ran to greet them, full of stories about his day, and then he sat between them in the four-wheel drive for the last short ride along from the Arnolds' house at the far end of the street to Drew's own place adjoining the medical centre.

'How about macaroni cheese for dinner?' Drew asked him.

'Yum!'

'Susan?'

'Sounds fine, and I'll make it.'

'No. . .'

'Please, Drew! You can——'

'Play with me!' Simon finished happily.

And so the scene half an hour later was alarmingly domestic. Susan pottered contentedly in the kitchen, thinking how nice it was to hear father's and son's voices in the next room. They all ate together, talking over their day, and the macaroni cheese was consumed by the two males with flattering enthusiasm. Afterwards, as she cleared up, Susan heard them in the bathroom, then came a quiet time as Simon had his bedtime story and was settled down for the night. It was just after eight o'clock when Drew emerged.

'Well. . .' he said, and their eyes met.

Susan had just come out of the kitchen and she felt like fleeing back there straight away. Kylie had gone. Simon was asleep. To all intents and purposes they were alone, and this was only the first such evening they would have to spend together.

She couldn't help remembering that kiss the other night. No! Stop! There hadn't been a kiss at all! Had Drew Kershaw got her so flustered that she couldn't even tell fantasy from reality any more? Now he parted his lips to speak, and she found that she was watching them and thinking once again of their pressure and warmth and how these things would feel against her own mouth.

He was wearing a khaki shirt, its sleeves rolled and its front splashed with some fading wetness from Simon's bath. She could see sinewy forearms and a strong collarbone disappearing inside the fabric and suddenly wanted to know much more about the shape and texture and scent of his body. . .

'I'm going to set up the stereo equipment,' he said. His compact discs and player had arrived yesterday in the crate that had carried Simon's toys as well. 'Some music would be nice, wouldn't it?'

'Yes,' she managed. 'It's so quiet here after the city.'

'Don't expect much for a couple of hours. I'm no electronics expert. It'll probably take me all evening.'

'Would a cup of tea help the process?' she suggested.

'Yes. Then I can sit back and take a few mouthfuls when I get to the point where I don't know what I'm doing!'

She laughed and disappeared into the kitchen again, extremely relieved to be alone to catch her breath for a few moments. Something very dangerous was happening inside her, and she didn't like or trust it at all.

I'm not going to develop some silly crush on him! she thought. I've *never* been that type! We have to work together, and for the moment we have to live together. That's no big deal, and it's going to be as sensible as possible!

Having made the tea, she sat on the couch to drink it and took out the novel she had been reading over the past few days. Chapter nine, wasn't it, where the heroine discovered that. . .? No, it was the heroine's *sister*. . . She flipped back and forth for several minutes before she found the right place, distracted by her determination *not* to watch Drew carefully unpacking his equipment.

He had been too self-deprecating about his skill at electronics. Half an hour later, soft music swelled into the room and he sank into an armchair to listen critically, then with growing appreciation, to the sound. Susan put her book down. Really, the plot was very thin, and she couldn't keep track of the characters at all. . .

The compact disc must have lasted for nearly three quarters of an hour, and in that time neither of them moved. Susan was almost frightened to do so, lest it shatter a sense of peace and contentment that she couldn't remember ever having felt before. As for

Drew. . . She didn't know why he was sitting back so
lazily in that chair with his green eyes half closed and
scarcely visible through those two thick fans of lashes.
Perhaps he was just tired.

His arm was draped along the arm of the chair so
that it created just the right curved shape for someone
to nestle in, and again she could imagine so vividly
what it would be like to be that person, to feel that
warm body against hers, undulating very slightly with
the rise and fall of his breathing. When the music
ended at last, she had to shake off the image immediately by standing to say, 'I think I'll have a quick
shower. My skin still smells of chlorine after our swim
today.'

He only nodded, and as she went down the corridor
she heard a new disc beginning—this time with a
rhythmic beat and an insistent rock melody, as if he
was trying to shake off the mood created by his
previous choice. It was a quarter to ten when she
emerged from the bathroom wearing a cream cotton
nightdress and pastel-toned kimono.

Early for bed, but. . . Music still sounded from the
living-room and she wanted to avoid Drew. Taking her
book, she tucked herself into bed, became absorbed in
the story at last and must have dozed, as the next thing
she was aware of was that her right arm had gone numb
and her left forefinger was wedged into the spine of the
open book.

The house was quiet now. Drew must have gone to
bed too. How late was it? Nine o'clock, according to
her watch. She had forgotten to wind it. Thirsty, and
with watch in hand, Susan padded down to the kitchen
in her bare feet, not bothering with the kimono this
time. Five past eleven, and that bottled spring water,
chilled from the fridge, tasted good. . .

Drew, emerging from the bathroom with wet, towel-
rumpled hair, a bare chest and legs clad in navy silk
pyjama-pants, didn't notice the light clicking off in the

kitchen. He assumed that by this time little Miss
Carstairs was safely asleep. She had got under his skin
again tonight, sitting there so dreamily as she let the
music wash over her. They had both sat far too still on
their chastely separate couch and armchair, as if any
movement at all was too dangerously sensual, and he
had begun to think that there was something to be said,
after all, for the old-fashioned custom of chaperonage.
Some dragon of a dowager beside her on that couch
would have taken the heat out of the atmosphere. . .

Here she was. She had been in the kitchen and now
she was coming towards him. What was she carrying?
Her watch. He recognised the plain brown band. And
her surprise at seeing him was as great as his at seeing
her, that was clear. She gasped and her cream nightdress seemed to tremble. It was, as he would have
expected, a virginal garment with its elbow-length
sleeves and wide round neck edged in lace, no hint of
décolletage or transparency.

None the less, he was suddenly far too conscious of
the slim yet quite adequately curved figure beneath,
just suggested by a whispering outline of form and
contour as she moved reluctantly towards him.

'I was thirsty,' Susan explained to Drew's bare
chest—although 'bare' didn't seem quite the word for
an expanse of bronzed and lightly freckled skin that
was so thoroughly roughened by curls of dark hair.

If only she had seen the light shining beneath the
bathroom door, she could have scurried back to her
room and waited until he had disappeared safely into
his own bedroom. Now there was no choice but to pass
him with a breathlessly murmured apology, and the
corridor suddenly seemed too narrow. He would think
she was crazy, a real mouse of a creature, if she pressed
herself back against the opposite wall as she wanted to
do, so when she did slip past him, keeping firmly to her
course, she felt her nightdress brush and drag against
those silk pyjama-pants.

'Susan?'

'Yes?'

She stopped and turned, tilting her face up to him so that their eyes met. He raised a hand very slowly and stretched soft fingers towards her jawline while she stood motionless, waiting for his touch. She could feel his warmth, smell the almond scent of his shampoo, and if she had swayed just a few inches closer to him her breasts and thighs would have touched him through the two thin fabrics of cotton and silk. . .

His hand fell, and his touch was only a phantom promise that remained unfulfilled. 'Sleep well,' he said. 'Several tour groups arrive tomorrow, Jane told me, and the camping ground is fairly full. We may have some customers.'

'Mm-hmm. Sleep well yourself, then.'

She passed him at last, breathless and on fire, and couldn't sleep at all for a long time.

'Susan, are you dressed yet?'

'Just about. . .' Her fingers fumbled as she heard Drew's knock and his abrupt voice outside her bedroom door.

He wasn't in a very good mood this morning— taciturn and clearly preoccupied. Rising later than usual after her restless night, Susan had spent breakfast wrapped securely in her chaste kimono as she'd tried unsuccessfully to keep out of his way. She wasn't foolish enough to believe that their awareness of each other last night had anything to do with his mood now. He had probably quite forgotten about that, but she had heard him mutter at one point, more to himself than to her, 'Jane will take him for a bit longer, but that's no good. I'm building up a debt I can't repay. . .'

Susan's murmur of sympathy had been ignored. . . and now, as she tried to hurry in obedience to the command in his tone, the buttons on her blouse just would not fasten. She pulled and fiddled, and now one

of them was dangling by a few loose threads. She got it
at last, just as he said impatiently, 'Well, Margaret
Latham is here to introduce herself, so come out when
you're ready.'

'I am.' She emerged, a little breathless, and unsatis-
fied with the plain white blouse and cheap blue jeans.

'Good.' He strode out to the living-room and she
followed in his wake. 'Here she is, Margaret.' His tone
implied an added, At last!

'Hi! Hello!' said a bright voice. Margaret Latham
was energetic, streaky blonde and slim, and was very
smartly dressed in fashionably cut khaki trousers and a
jungle-print blouse.

'Hi. . .' Susan pulled self-consciously at her own
blouse, and the loose button came off in her hand. She
dropped it quickly into the pocket of her jeans and
hoped that no one had noticed.

'Would you like some coffee, Margaret?' Drew
asked, but the deputy ranger's wife shook her head.

'I haven't got time. I've left the baby with Matt and
she'll need feeding again soon. I've really come with a
business proposition, Drew.'

'Business?' he frowned.

'Yes and a toy for Simon.' She produced a small
metal car, Drew called his son, and the four-year-old
received the little present with delight and went off
immediately to play with it.

'Jane says he's a darling kid, and I can see she's
right,' Margaret said. The three adults listened for a
moment to the 'Vroom, vroom!' sounds that floated in
through the back door.

'Yes. . .' Drew's frown was more pronounced than
ever.

'We were up until midnight talking about him,'
Margaret went on.

'About Simon?' He stiffened.

'Yes, and Corey and Stacey, and Jeremy and Ben,
and little Neradee Yankunjarra, and my Laura. We've

been thinking of the idea for some time, but now we've got the incentive to actually get it started. We're going to run our own pre-school! And Simon, if you want, can be a full-time paying customer.'

'You mean. . .'

'We've all heard about Kylie running out on you. You must be feeling strapped. Let me tell you about it, and I think you'll find it's an answer.'

Twenty minutes later, Drew's face seemed to have lost several years' worth of tension. After listening to the outline of the plan and giving her approval, when appealed to eagerly by Margaret, Susan had excused herself to go and put some washing in the machine, make her untidy bed, and wash the breakfast dishes. She had caught snatches of enthusiastic talk as she worked, though.

'We'll be ordering play equipment from Perth, and we thought that you and the Shiptons might lend us some of the kids' own toys.'

'Sure! Simon's arrived the other day.'

'They'll be at Jane's in the mornings and my place in the afternoons.'

'And this Flora Mowanjum who works part-time at the motel. . .'

'Oh, she's delightful. Very responsible. A bit shy. Charming with children. She'd love the chance of some extra work looking after Simon when you're on call.'

'But listen, I've kept you far too long. You said you couldn't stay.'

'Yes, I must get back. Matt's probably frantic. Not to mention the baby. I'll just say goodbye to Susan.'

'I'm here, Margaret.' Susan emerged from the laundry-room.

'Did you know you've lost a button?' the other woman whispered as they came down the passage together.

'Oh, I know, yes.' Susan flushed. 'Most of my things are in the wash, so I couldn't change and I stupidly didn't bring a sewing kit up here. Not so much as a safety-pin!'

'Come round tonight and I'll sew it on for you.'

'No. . . I couldn't. . .'

'Oh, please! I'm hungry for someone new to work on.'

'Work on?'

'Yes. I love sewing and hair and fashion and there's so little opportunity for me to indulge in all that up here. I've made six outfits for the little Shipton twins, and I cut Lee and Jane's hair all the time. If you'll let me I'd like to *make* you a blouse instead of sewing that silly button back on. I've got two or three cotton print fabrics that'd look gorgeous on you. Please come!'

'I will,' Susan laughed. 'Strictly as a favour to you, mind, not because my wardrobe needs any work. I mean, can't you tell I had a fortune to spend on clothes before I came up here?'

'In other words, you need trousers and a dress as well. I thought so! I can't wait!'

Susan let Margaret out of the door, still laughing, and met Drew and Simon coming out of the little boy's room. 'It's almost too good to be true,' he said to her at once, not even bothering to explain that it was the pre-school idea he was talking about. He lowered his voice so that Simon, who was running ahead out of the back door, couldn't hear. 'I've been so knotted up about it. But Simon's already "best friends" with Jeremy. I couldn't be more pleased about how this has worked out.'

His face looked about five years younger when he was happy, Susan decided. That frown dropped away to reveal a forehead that was high and smooth and well-shaped. His top lip, which could look too thin at times, took on a very sensual fullness, and his smile was quite over-powering.

'We're going over to the Shiptons' store,' he said now. 'Simon needs some block-out cream.'

'We're running low on cheese, too,' she answered.

'I know, but can it wait? Tom is driving into Pendleton on Tuesday to do a big shop. He said he'll pick up a full complement of rations for us if we give him a list. Two months' worth, he suggested. I thought you and I could each work on suggestions separately, then compare notes. That way, we're less likely to forget something vital.'

'We might get some ideas from Jane, too,' Susan said. 'I've never had to plan two months' worth of grocery needs before.'

'Good idea. I'll do it on the way to the motel.'

He and Simon were gone for quite a while, and, foolishly, she missed them as she hummed about the house, making herself a cup of freshly brewed, inky dark coffee at about eleven and cleaning the kitchen sink and stove. It was *very* foolish to miss them. 'I'd just like to see him smiling like that again!'

But when she did hear Drew and his son coming home. . .

'Stop flopping about in that silly way!' It was noon, and Susan was hanging her washing out on the line.

The boy and his father were approaching the back door, hand in hand. Drew's expression was grim and the little boy was indeed dragging his feet, staggering about and giggling in quite a maddening fashion. Susan pretended not to notice the altercation that followed, but of course she could hear every word.

'It's time for your lunch, so what would you like? A sandwich?'

'I'm not hungry.'

'Yes, I shouldn't have given you that peppermint chocolate five minutes ago, should I?'

'Yes, you should. I want more!'

'There isn't any more.'

'Yes, there is. What's in your pocket?'

'Not chocolate. Block-out cream.'

'Chocolate.'

'No more chocolate. Lunch!'

'I'm *not hungry*!'

'Well, it's my own fault, I suppose.' There was a defeated sigh. 'Go and play in your room for a while and we'll have lunch later.'

Drew coaxed the child firmly up the back steps and Simon seemed to obey without further difficulty, then the doctor turned to see Susan hanging up a towel and last week's uniform on the rotary clothes-line. Hesitating for a second or two, he then came back down the steps and strode across to her, breaking into frustrated speech immediately.

'He was fine at Jane's. But at the Shiptons'. . . He went off with the twins and all three of them got over-excited and giggly. Stacey and Corey like to "help" Flora Mowanjum do the rooms, apparently. She'll be looking after Simon sometimes, as you heard, so it was good that the two of them got to meet each other. But I can just imagine how much help he was this morning. The chocolate was a bribe, and I thought it would settle him, but on the way back he got worse and worse!'

'Go and throw a few rocks till you calm down,' Susan advised, daring to adopt a teasing tone.

'I think I will!'

He strode into the house and Susan followed a minute or two later, to find him rather grimly at work making sandwiches in the kitchen. She helped him, and when they were ready she asked, 'Do you think Simon will have got his appetite back yet?'

'He'll come looking for food if he has. I'm not going to make a scene over it.'

'He's been as quiet as a mouse in his room, hasn't he?'

'Mmm. Too quiet, perhaps.' The frown was back again. 'I'd better check on him.'

'I'll do it,' she offered quickly, feeling an oddly protective urge towards this man who was so uncomfortable in his role as a father.

She rose before he could protest, and went along the corridor, only to stop abruptly in the doorway of the child's room. He was flung out on his back on the bed, fast asleep, his little cheeks a dark rose colour and his breathing heavy and slow.

'Little sweetie!' she murmured, and tiptoed back to Drew.

But the latter frowned at her report. 'That's odd,' he said. 'He hardly ever sleeps in the day now, according to Kate, and never this early. He slept later than usual this morning, too, so he shouldn't be tired. I hope he isn't. . .'

He got up, leaving his half-finished sandwich, and Susan followed him along the corridor once again. Simon's cheeks seemed even pinker now, and his breathing loud and sluggish in rhythm. Drew bent down and shook him gently. 'Simon?'

No response.

'Simon?' Now it was more urgent, but still the boy didn't even stir, although his mouth fell slackly open.

Drew was no longer looking at the little face, though. He had reached for Simon's wrist and was taking his pulse with one hand while the other felt the boy's skin in several places. 'He's not feverish, and yet it *isn't* normal sleep. Can you see any bites, Susan? Take a close look, while I——?' Then he said, interrupting himself, 'But surely if he was bitten by anything unusual he would have told me at once!'

Susan squeezed gently past Drew towards the head of the bed, and began to examine the boy's neck and hair for any signs of a bite. Drew's knee pressed heavily into her thigh as he lifted Simon's cotton T-shirt to check his abdomen.

'The symptoms don't fit,' he murmured.

They didn't, but Susan straightened now and faced Simon's father as light dawned. 'He hasn't been bitten, Drew,' she said. 'He's drunk.'

CHAPTER FIVE

'WHAT?' Drew heard his own voice as if it belonged to someone else, sounding strangled and thunderous at the same time.

'On his breath,' Susan said. 'I smelt it as I bent over him. The peppermint chocolate probably masked it for you before. Beer, I think.'

He moved her aside and bent towards Simon's face. 'You're right. How on earth. . .?' He shook the boy again, even as he fought to suppress his rising anger, and this time there was a childish groan and a mumble. 'How much could he have had? It was half-empty beer cans from the motel rooms this morning, I suppose. Lee Shipton said two lots of guests had been pretty rowdy last night. . . We should get him to vomit if we can, although most of the stuff must already be absorbed.'

A miserable fifteen minutes followed. They managed to waken the child at last, and then there was no need for syrup of ipecacuanha. Simon did it all on his own. He remained groggy and confused and complained of a headache, but refused to down the aspirin and water that Susan proffered.

Through all this, Drew fought a losing battle with his anger. Those flushed cheeks, that sour breath. . .

Drew had never liked the sight of a man drunk, and it was worse to see a child this way. Craig Osborne had always been a drinker, and an unpleasant one. It was one of the reasons why Drew had almost refused to believe, at first, that the man was Lisa's lover. Craig Osborne? Of the loud laughter, the coarse jokes, the wandering hands and the same sour breath that Simon had now? Impossible! But Lisa had convinced him—

81

oh, yes, convinced him utterly!—and he had felt like a fool, and worse, for not guessing before.

'*Should* I have guessed?'

But if he had guessed what would have changed? Very little. And certainly not this terrible anger that had seized hold of him now at the sight of Simon in a drunken stupor, Simon messily losing the remains of his breakfast and that ill-timed chocolate, Simon clutching a pounding head with a wince and a grimace just like the one Craig Osborne might have worn after a heavy night. . .

His fist tingled with a violent impulse, and a terrible, nauseating fear of his own strength mingled with his anger to form a lethal cocktail of feeling.

Simon moaned and cried, and Drew made out the words, 'I want to ring Aunty Kate. I want Aunty Kate to be here. . .'

'I can't stand this!' he ground out abruptly through teeth that were clenched so hard they hurt. 'I'm going out for a walk up Wingoona Gorge. You'll have to deal with it. Sorry.'

He had gone before Susan could even find a reply.

'I feel awful,' Simon sobbed seconds later.

No wonder! thought Susan. Your father just abandoned you in a white rage. *I* feel awful about it too! Aloud, her face revealing nothing of her thoughts, she said gently, 'I know you do, love. Please have the aspirin and the water and you'll feel better soon.'

'Will I?'

'I promise. Lots of water, and some more sleep. Beer is pretty strong stuff, you see, even for big people. I don't like it myself. And for little boys it's just awful!'

'We were just playing a game.'

'I know you were, and now you know not to do it again.'

At last the aspirin was downed and Susan cajoled as much liquid into him as she could, knowing that dehydration was what accounted for the worst of the hangover symptoms. She suggested something to eat as well, but Simon only shook his head miserably and she did not force the issue. The poor little chap! As she tucked him into bed and closed his curtains against the bright daylight, she heard him say again, 'I want Aunty Kate to be here. . .' but it would be another six months before this wish could be fulfilled.

His resilience in this new world had been amazing, with the drama over Kylie and now this. . .'We'll ring her again tonight, shall we?' Susan promised soothingly on Drew's behalf, and the little face relaxed until his eyes closed and he slept.

Drew had been gone for two hours when the buzzer sounded beside the phone, signalling a radio call. Simon had just woken, feeling better but still clearly fuddled and listless. Susan had made him a sandwich and given him as much liquid as he would drink.

Now she didn't know what to do and was furious at the boy's father. How could you blame a four-year-old for drinking too much beer? Clearly it had just been a curious child's mistake. And how could you stride off into the shimmering outback day without any word about when you might be back?

This was meant to be *my* time! Susan fumed inwardly. And I've been wrong to let the man soften me up so easily! I don't believe that Lisa's death excuses the way he treats Simon.

The fact that she had wanted Drew's kiss so badly last night did nothing to appease her. If anything, it made her feel worse. I'm far too naïve, she decided. He probably did it deliberately. . .

And now there might be an emergency, she didn't know where to contact Flora Mowanjum, Simon's new baby-sitter, no one was answering the phone at the Arnolds' or the Lathams', and Drew Kershaw was completely out of contact.

'We have to go next door,' she told Simon as she got

the medical centre keys. 'There's a call for us on the radio.'

The child's face brightened as he sensed excitement, and he wasn't wrong. Her hands dampening as she tackled the still unfamiliar equipment, Susan managed to give the correct opening words and then heard Tom Arnold's voice, deceptively laconic and calm.

'Hello, Susan, do you read me? Over.'

'Reading you loud and clear, Tom. Over.'

'We've got an accident up here in Tanamee Gorge. A hiker. Fall of about six or eight metres. Could be serious, but we don't want to move him till the doc takes a look. Over.'

'That's right, Tom, don't move him if there's any chance at all of spinal injury. But Drew's not here. . .'

'Yes, I am.'

She had left the door open and he entered at a stride to take over the controls. 'More detail, please, Tom. How long has he been there? Is there any bleeding? Don't move him in any circumstances, and keep him warm. I'll call the Flying Doctor, and we'll be on our way as soon as possible.'

A few minutes later they had bundled some equipment into the back of the four-wheel drive and were ready to start. 'Simon will have to come,' Drew decreed in a rough undertone to Susan. 'There isn't time to see if Flora can look after him, and besides he's only met her once. Sit with him in the back, would you?'

'OK.' She didn't bother to pretend to a warmth she no longer felt, and caught his startled glance and awakening comprehension. If he knows why I'm angry, so much the better, she decided.

Their journey was a rough one. Long, too. Drew cursed under his breath at each pothole and each unpredictable twist in the track. The landscape in this section of the park was spectacular. Square-cut blocks of ancient, weathered stone ranging in hue from rust-red to cream to golden-brown, and almost to purple in some lights, rose all around them, the contours softened by desert plants such as spinifex and the vividly named poached-egg daisies.

The party of hikers who had come out this way yesterday were intrepid and experienced, camping overnight in a small gully before crossing over more rocky terrain to reach the natural amphitheatre that was Tanamee Falls. It was here that disaster had struck. Clambering over loose rock, one of the party had fallen and now lay crumpled on the ground, in pain and with the extent of his injuries unknown.

When they arrived, after half an hour of jolting battle with the road, Matt Latham stepped out into a clearing and pointed to the parking spot he had cleared for them. Easy access to the rear of the vehicle was important, as the patient would have to be transported in the back of the four-wheel drive to meet the Flying Doctor plane at the airstrip.

'Tom's up there with them,' Matt reported. 'I'll have to show you the way. It's not easy to find the route up, although you can see the spot from here. It's only two hundred metres or so, but. . .' He glanced uneasily at the child in the back seat.

'Simon, you'll have to wait in the car,' Drew said gruffly.

Susan glared at the doctor and, with satisfaction, watched him colour. 'Read the stories we brought, love,' she told him. 'And give a toot on the horn every few minutes. That's very important, OK? It'll cheer up the poor man that's fallen. Here. . .climb over into the front seat so you can reach it.'

He did so, distracted now from any fear he might have felt at being left alone.

Drew threw her a grateful glance but she refused to acknowledge it, still far too angry with him. They pulled equipment from the rear of the vehicle and set off, hearing the first of Simon's toots only a minute or two later. The sound was reassuring to all of them. The climb was arduous, and would be treacherous on the way down, with a patient on a stretcher to transport. Matt Latham, with his shock of thick, sandy hair, looked strong, and so was Drew. Hopefully they were both sure-footed as well.

Halfway up, they met two of the hikers in the party, who were heading down to the vehicle track carrying the injured man's camping equipment as well as their own.

'We've left my. . .my son in our four-wheel drive,' Drew told them, with an abruptness that was characteristic whenever he spoke of Simon. 'He's a brave kid, but he'll be a bit lonely, so can you tell him everything is OK?'

'Sure!' said the man and woman in unison, then the latter added,

'We've got a snack to eat too—raisins and nuts and oranges. He'd like to share some, wouldn't he?'

'I'm sure he would.'

A few more minutes of climbing brought them to the site of the accident, and Susan shuddered when she looked up and saw how far the hiker must have fallen. He lay half wedged between two giant red rocks, with Tom Arnold and the other three hikers grouped anxiously around him. Fully conscious, he was white with pain and trembled beneath the sleeping-bag that had been laid on top of him to guard against heat loss through shock.

Everyone stepped back as Drew approached, and he dropped to his haunches beside the injured hiker. 'Did you hit your head?'

'I don't think so,' the man mouthed through pale, dry lips. 'It's my left leg. . .'

'We'll check all the same.' He checked the man's airway, breathing and circulation, examined his skull for external damage, checked for limb weakness, unequal pupil dilation and other signs of head injury, then sat back a little, and began to question him. 'What's your name?'

'Paul Giddens. But. . .'

'And what day of the week is it?'

'Sunday.'

'And who's the prime minister this month?'

Susan suppressed a smile, but Paul Giddens made an angry sound, gave the correct answer, then said, 'But what the hell. . .? My leg is killing me.'

'How many fingers am I holding up?'

'Three.'

'And can you follow this one with your eyes?'

Drew pursued his questions relentlessly, in spite of the man's increasing anger, and Susan knew why. The leg might be by far the most painful and obvious injury, but cranial or spinal damage was much more serious. Finally the doctor was satisfied, although both the spine and neck would be immobilised with a wooden board for the journey back to the vehicle, to the airstrip, and by plane to hospital in Pendleton.

'Looks as if you've been lucky, Paul,' he told the man a short while later. 'Odds are good that everything is intact. Susan?'

'Yes?'

He spoke to her in a low tone. 'Fracture of the femur. Nothing else that I can see, but that doesn't rule out a slow subdural bleed that may show up later on, or a loose chip of bone somewhere in that spine that could compromise the spinal cord.'

'Unlikely, though. . .'

'Unlikely,' he agreed. 'But frightening out here where we don't have X-ray equipment to check it on the spot.'

'I know. After the kind of hospital we're both used to. . .'

'We'll have to splint the leg on the spot and use the portable traction device, too, because the thigh muscles are forcing the broken bones to overlap. Prepare me that morphine, would you? And erythromycin orally. That open wound is very likely to become infected. Swab any grazes and gashes with antiseptic. He's lost some blood. We'll set up an IV to replace fluids more quickly. . .'

The two of them set to work, with Tom Arnold's help needed as well when it came to splinting and putting the leg in traction. Then came the arduous descent by stretcher and the painfully rough ride in the four-wheel drive. Susan crouched beside the injured hiker in the back of the vehicle, forgetting her cramped and uncomfortable position as she constantly monitored his condition. The symptoms of shock were not yet diminishing despite the intravenous fluids and medication that had been given. This man needed a hospital, with oxygen, an X-ray machine and quiet, clean conditions.

Drew was all too aware of this as well. His driving was skilled and tension-filled as he constantly balanced the need for speed with the need to keep the patient as comfortable as possible. Beside him sat Simon, too overwhelmed by the drama and by his father's gritty expression to speak at all.

Poor kid, Susan had time to think halfway through the journey. He doesn't realise that Drew is totally intent on saving this man. Simon thinks those clenched teeth still mean anger against him. . .

It was very late when they finally arrived back at the house. The Flying Doctor plane had made a successful take-off and already Paul Giddens would be receiving oxygen, more fluids and another dose of pain medication. He should make a full recovery. . .

'Tinned soup and toast for dinner, I think,' Drew decreed, and Susan nodded.

'The quicker the better, too. Simon is tired.'

'Listen. . .' Drew lowered his voice as they stood in the living-room. Simon, still very subdued, had gone to investigate the compact disc collection, which con-

tained several sets of children's songs and narrated
stories. 'I'm not hungry yet, and I have to wind up
some things from this afternoon. Phone ahead to the
hospital and the Flying Doctor base, and so forth.
Could you feed Simon and put him to bed? It's a big
favour. I know, but——'

'No, Drew!' She faced him, very firm and strong with
the anger that had been smouldering in her ever since
lunch-time. 'I'll feed him, sure, but his bedtime can
wait until you've finished.' She continued in an even
lower tone, 'Can't you see how much he needs you
after today? After this whole week, frankly! Surely I
don't need to go into details! And you had no cause to
be angry with him about what he did this morning. It
was——'

'I know,' he growled. 'You don't need to go on. I
behaved unforgivably. I'll. . . I'll put him to bed and
we'll talk. I'll tell him I'm sorry.'

'Good.' His immediate agreement took the wind out
of her sails and left her uneasy at the same time.

Something was eating at him, torturing him, and
Simon was suffering because of it. Drew clearly knew
it far better than she did. Perhaps having the child live
with Kate and Charles Kershaw, which Susan had at
first seen as abandonment, was the best thing he could
have done for him. . .

Drew went next door to the medical centre and
Susan asked Simon to choose between the three different soups they had in stock. Chicken noodle was the
predictable winner, and both of them had eaten by the
time Drew returned.

With a reluctance that Susan prayed the boy did not
see, he escorted Simon to bed, spending nearly an hour
in the little bedroom, while murmured voices crept
under the closed door. Then he returned to the kitchen
to prowl around as he waited for toast to pop up and
soup to reheat. When it was done, he did not bother

with the formality of the table, but came into the living-room and sat down in the blue-grey armchair.

Susan had been doing her needlework—a delicate tablecloth in drawn thread work which she would probably never have the remotest use for, but which satisfied some creative craving in her soul none the less. Unfortunately, even the precise details of the needlecraft didn't take up the whole of her mind, and as she worked she had been aware of Drew's every movement.

She looked up as he spoke to her. 'I suppose you'd like to hear a report from the Flying Doctor Service on our patient?'

A polite affirmation rose to her lips. . .and died there as it was overtaken at last by the anger and helplessness she had been bottling inside her all day.

'No, Drew, I wouldn't,' she told him, throwing her fancy work carelessly aside. She had startled him, that was clear. Now she had to go on. 'I want to hear the truth about you and Simon.'

'What? I——'

'Look, we're going to be sharing this place for several more weeks, and I've reached my limit already. Your anger was cruel today, cruel and dangerous, and I can't stand by and——'

She stopped, and she was crying, he saw at once. She didn't try to hide it as many women would have, nor to play it for all it was worth as Lisa always had. Instead, she just stood there—when had she got up from the couch?—facing him and letting the tears stream out of those brown eyes and sobs shake those neat, firm shoulders.

'Oh, hell, Susan!'

The desire he had felt for her since Wednesday night melted into a feeling of immense tenderness, and he pulled her into his arms to cradle her brown head against his shoulder as he listened to the jerky phrases that poured forth. It took him some seconds to realise that she was *apologising*.

'I'm sorry. . . I have no right, I suppose, but. . . My father made it so clear how. . .*unwanted* I was after my mother's death. At first because he. . .couldn't cope with caring for a child, I think, and then because he married again. My aunt brought me up. She meant well. . .but she was too old, fifteen years older than my mother, and too set in her ways for the job.'

'Susan. . .'

'Do you know. . .' she tried to laugh, that low, full-bodied laugh that was so surprising and so delightful, but it had a strangled note now and was more like a sob '. . .I still can't stand to have a clock ticking in the house because Aunty Dot had so many of them? And she didn't like music, you see, so I grew up to the rhythm of twelve clocks going tick-tock, tick-tock every minute of the day. I was lonely and different and unwanted, and I can't stand by and see. . .another child. . .' She couldn't go on, although she kept trying.

He tried to convince her that it didn't matter, that she had said enough, and somehow the only way he could do this was to keep holding her, caressing her back, nuzzling the top of her head with his lips, stroking damp strands of hair out of those brown eyes and, finally, kissing that trembling mouth as he now admitted fully to himself that he had been aching to do for days.

Her response, at first, was as innocent as he had known it would be. Her lips, still trembling slightly, were as tender and tentative as if she were nibbling on some strange new fruit, and the little sounds she made in her throat were kitten-like. His own ardour and urgency threatened to build with frightening speed and he had to hold back until he felt her lips part. . .

Susan tasted him and couldn't put a name to the sensation at all. Her insides were swelling, fluttering, melting, and her hands had taken on a life of their own as they massaged his back with sensuous, rhythmic movements. She wanted to stay like this forever because it seemed that she would never know enough about his kiss to satisfy her. The way his nose gently bumped hers. The way whispered words. . .the sound of her name. . .brushed against her lips as he drew away a little and then returned to plunder her mouth more deeply. The way his hands imprisoned her, first jaw and throat, then waist and hips, then breasts. . .

'Susan we have to stop.'

'No, we don't.' She didn't think about the import of the words at all.

'Yes, we *do*!'

'Why? I——'

'Because it isn't fair. I'm a man, and there's only one way this can end in satisfaction for me.'

'And I'm a woman, Drew.'

'Are you?' He searched the innocent eagerness of her gaze.

'If you mean in *that way*, then no,' she told him in a low voice.

'I thought not.' Then, as she shrank away from him, 'Listen! I didn't mean that as an attack. I meant. . . This isn't how it should happen for you! You need——'

'Don't tell me what I need!' She looked up, met his eyes steadily and saw that, with this gesture, she had at least commanded his respect. 'OK, you're right. Like you, my body seems to have its own priorities, but they don't fit with what's sensible, do they?'

'No, they don't,' he growled, his voice still blurred with the aftermath of desire. 'I'm glad you see that too.'

It wasn't necessary to spell it out in words. His maturity, her youth. His jaded experience of marriage, her rosy dreams. The fact that they worked together and lived beneath the same roof.

'So this is business that will remain unfinished,' he told her. 'There's something else, though. . .'

'Is there?' She had almost forgotten how this whole thing had started.

'What you said. . .about me and Simon.'

'Oh, yes. . .'

'Let's go outside.'

He took her hand and led the way. On the veranda the air was cool, and it felt good as it fanned her cheeks. After the drama of the day, she was tired. . . He sat down beside her on the steps and for a few minutes they were both silent, just looking out into the star-filled, velvet-skied outback night. Drew was the one to break the silence, and the words spilled jaggedly from his lips with all the urgency and awkwardness of a long-held secret.

'Simon isn't my son.'

The simple sentence seemed to echo in the desert silence. 'He's adopted?' she asked hesitantly.

'No! He's Lisa's child, and until he was fourteen months old I thought he was mine, but then she told me the truth. He was fathered by her lover. By Craig.'

'No!'

'It's not the sort of thing you're used to, is it?' he ground out. 'I'm sorry, but some marriages do contain some pretty sordid secrets.'

'But, Drew, it's impossible. He *looks* like you!'

'Does he?' It was accompanied by a hard, cynical smile.

'Yes! Not his colouring, I know, but his expressions sometimes, his gestures.'

'It's funny, isn't it?' he answered slowly and with a bitter thoughtfulness. 'People are always determined to see a resemblance between a parent and a child. Strangers who thought that Simon belonged to Charles and Kate told *her* that he had exactly her nose, or her chin. And of course Simon and Kate aren't blood relatives at all.'

'That's true,' Susan had to admit. 'I think it happens to adoptive parents too.'

There was a small silence, then he went on, 'She told me the night she left to go with Craig. Didn't so much *tell* me, but *flung* it at me like some trump card she had been hoarding up. I hadn't even suspected that she was Craig's lover until that night. And to find it out in that way! Her cruelty. . .it was mind-boggling.'

'But. . .did you ask for proof that he wasn't yours?'

'Proof? I didn't need proof. The whole thing made far too much sense. It was why our marriage had gone sour so soon. Hell, I must have been quite blind! It made me so sick, I——'

'You found you couldn't love him any more. . .' she whispered, appalled at the bitterness of his words.

'No! That's the hell of it. You don't stop loving a child you've known from the moment he was born just because of some abstract issue of biological fatherhood. It would have been a lot easier if I *could* have stopped loving him.'

'You still blame him, though. . .'

'I don't blame him,' he muttered. 'Don't be ridiculous!'

'Then what, Drew? I *want* to understand!' Wanted it more urgently than she had wanted anything for a long time, even his kiss.

She saw his struggle for words, expressed in the tight hunch of his shoulders and in the jerky, repetitive movements of the stick he fiddled with, scratching it in the red dirt at the bottom of the steps. But she was wise enough not to prod or prompt now, and sat waiting for his answer with her eyes combing over every detail of his strained face.

'I—I felt that night as if I could have killed Craig if I'd been given the chance. I'd never known such rage before. I threw things, smashed things—Lisa's photo, the china on the mantelpiece. I almost broke my fists, I think, smashing them into doors and walls, and all the time it was Craig's face I was seeing. I'm not proud of those feelings.'

'Normal, though, don't you think?' she told him gently.

'Perhaps. It scares me, though. I'd never thought of myself as an animal before, but that night I was. And again today. I felt that same rage against Simon. It's what I've been afraid of, why I've tried to distance myself, why I put him in the hands of Kate and Charles where he was safe. And now he's torn, missing them, loving me even when I can't respond to him.'

'Kate and Charles know all of this, of course. . . .'

'They don't. They've never doubted that Simon is mine. Like me, you see, they didn't suspect about the affair. You're the only person I've ever told.'

'Oh. . .'

Neither of them wanted to explore why this might be so. There was another silence, then Susan ventured, 'But with time, Drew, won't it get better? You love Simon for himself, and he's innocent in this.'

'But what if, with time, it gets worse?' he ground out. 'Before I ever knew that Craig was Lisa's lover I disliked the kind of man he was. Loud, loutish, flashy in his good looks and in his way of spending money, a heavy, irresponsible drinker. Heredity still counts for a certain amount in a person's make-up, you know. I love Simon.' His voice choked on the words. 'But what if I see him turning into a boy like Craig must have been? What if one day I see my wife's lover looking out of that boy's face, and I *can't* restrain my anger or walk away from it as I did today?'

It was unanswerable, and any assurance she could have tried to give him would have carried no weight. She didn't know him well enough. She didn't know any man well enough to be able to say, No, at the last moment you wouldn't let yourself. I believe in you.

This left her with nothing to say at all. Since he too seemed to have no further words, they sat beside each other on the veranda steps in painful silence for a long time. . .

CHAPTER SIX

'MM, YOU'RE long-waisted,' said Margaret Latham. 'I thought you might be. Lucky I allowed the extra two inches on this bodice. OK, now turn around and I'll pin the other side.'

Susan pivoted obediently and rather cautiously, as the right side-seam of the blouse was only pinned as well. It was a Wednesday afternoon, five o'clock, and Margaret had come over 'for a fitting' as she phrased it.

'I feel like a model at Christian Dior,' Susan laughed.

'And you'll look like one, too, when I've finished with you,' Margaret retorted. 'We'll cut your hair soon, but I haven't worked out what to do with it yet.'

'I'd like something that keeps it off my neck,' Susan told her.

'Practical creature, aren't you?'

'Not always. . .'

'We can do much better than just keeping it off your neck. And you really do have a lovely figure. I'm envious.'

'Oh, rubbish! Look at you! Not an ounce of fat anywhere.'

'But it's a struggle. Especially when I love cake and ice-cream so much.'

'You manage to resist them, though.'

'Well. . . I do have a secret weapon that neutralises those calorie bombs. Without that, I'd be as fat as a pork barrel.' She gave a rather smug, secretive smile. 'Now, lift your arms. . .'

She put several pins in her mouth then took them out one by one to fasten the left side of the blouse, and Susan was left wondering, Secret weapon? She didn't like the sound of the phrase, somehow. Did Margaret over-use laxatives or diet pills in order to keep her slim shape? That could be dangerous. But the attractive and energetic thirty-two-year-old looked healthy and bright-eyed with her expertly streaked hair and emerald-green eyes. Susan decided that she was reading too much into an innocent phrase.

At that moment, Simon and Drew trooped in.

'Bathtime, kid,' the latter was saying. 'I don't know how you attract dirt the way you do. . .'

'I like it,' the child returned indignantly. 'When I'm a bigger boy, I'm going to be dirty *all the time*!'

'I bet you are!'

'Can we ring Aunty Kate and tell her about the house we made for the lizard?'

'Aunty Kate? Sure. . .'

Susan just had time to catch the expression of complicated love in Drew's face before they disappeared in the direction of the bathroom.

A week had now passed since the night of their kiss and of the doctor's revelations to her as they sat together afterwards on the veranda steps. Since then, neither of them had mentioned the subject. The next day, Drew had been. . .not cool towards her, but distant and wary, as if expecting some embarrassing or hostile response. But Susan had realised at once what he was feeling.

No one likes to face someone they've just confided in, she knew. He probably wishes he had held his tongue. . .but I'm glad he didn't. It explains so much. . .

She tried to show him all this—not through words but through her manner. At work, she was professionally courteous and friendly, while at home she was less formal, and teased him quite a bit, a little surprised at herself for daring to do so. It seemed to work. The wariness gradually disappeared, at any rate,

to be replaced in both of them by a very civilised
goodwill.

As for their kiss. . .it might never have been. Certainly she thought that no third person would guess
that they had ever been locked together in a passion-
ately sensual embrace. It wouldn't happen again.

All for the best, she told herself. We both know
that.

This did not mean that her awareness of him had
died away. How could it, with the daily intimacy of
living under the same roof? That would end soon,
though. Susan's new house was moving daily towards
completion, furniture and household utensils had
already been delivered. They were currently stored
under well-secured tarpaulins on the back veranda of
the medical centre, so there would be no last-minute
hold-ups in that area.

Meanwhile she was acquiring some new clothes for
the as yet unstarted built-in wardrobes.

'You can put your arm down again, dear,' Margaret
drawled, and Susan wondered how long she had been
standing like an odd sort of sculpture, lost in thought.

There was the sound of a vehicle outside at that
moment, and the other woman muttered, 'That's not
Matt stopping to pick me up, is it? He was going up for
a swim at Wingoona waterhole with the baby, but he
shouldn't be back yet. I can't hear Laura crying. . .'

'No, it's not Matt,' Susan said, craning her neck out
of the window.

A dusty four-wheel drive had pulled up untidily in
front of the medical centre, and a man was getting out.

'Drew, I think you'd better come,' Susan called. She
could see, even from this distance, the makeshift
bandages made of handkerchiefs and towelling on the
man's right arm, chest and face, and his stiff movements as he walked towards the centre showed that he
was in pain.

'What is it?'

'An accident of some kind. I don't know. . .'

'That's Brian Hamilton from Namburra Downs,' Margaret came in.

'He's definitely hurt.'

'Yes.' Drew had appeared now. 'Let's get going, Susan. Why on earth didn't he radio or phone to say he was coming in? Simon?'

He strode back to the bathroom as Susan disappeared into her room to remove the pinned blouse carefully and slip into her uniform.

'Yes, Daddy?' She could hear their voices as she changed.

'I have to go, little boy.'

'And I'm going to finish your bath with you,' Margaret said.

'I'll ring Flora now. At this time of day, she should be able to come up straight away.'

'Flora? She's so fun!' Simon exclaimed. 'Will she come in the bath?'

'Not *in* the bath, my lad.'

'When will you be back, Daddy?'

'Don't know yet. But I'll only be next door if you need me badly.'

'Can I still ring Aunty Kate? Flora can do the number for me.'

'Yes, you can still ring Aunty Kate.'

'Hurray! Hurray! Hurray! But I love you the best, Daddy,' he suddenly added, his voice dropping with gruff concern.

'Do you, Simon?' There was an odd, foggy note in Drew's voice now. 'That's. . .that's good.' Susan, emerging from her room again, saw the heavy in-breath expanding his strong chest. 'I love you too, little boy.'

Less than a minute later they were both striding towards the medical centre. 'Your sewing session is spoiled,' Drew said.

'We've almost finished.'

'Now. . .'

The man who came agitatedly towards them was a typical outback cattle farmer—solidly built, leathery brown, with stoicism reflected in every muscle. 'Brian Hamilton,' he said now, trying to put out his uninjured left hand to be shaken.

But Drew Kershaw wasn't wasting any time. 'You're burnt,' he said as he unlocked the building and led the way straight to the surgery. 'Let's get you stripped off a bit and see how bad it is. Why on earth did you drive over here by yourself, man?'

'I was down at the Seven-Mile Creek paddock. No one with me. Radio out for repairs. Stupid, really. Radiator boiled and I didn't wait long enough to take off the cap. She blew in my face, steam and boiling water. Crikey, it hurts!' His teeth were clenched, and he was shaking and sweating now. 'It was quicker to driver straight here myself than backtrack to the homestead. How did you know it was burns?'

'They're scattered, and you didn't cover them all with those dressings. The marks are in a splash pattern. How clean was the handkerchief and the towel?'

'Hankie was clean. Towel. . .sort of.'

'Hmm.' Drew nodded, his eyes narrowed. 'Susan, get a dressing tray. We need to clean these. I'm going to put in an IV to replace fluids, and he'll need morphine and antibiotics.'

He named drug types and doses, and Susan nodded as Brian Hamilton came in, alarmed, 'Morphine?'

'This isn't going to stop hurting in an hour or two, Mr Hamilton. In fact, it's going to get worse. . .'

It did, although the cattleman's stoicism almost disguised the fact. Drew diagnosed partial thickness burns to five per cent of Brian Hamilton's skin surface. The small percentage meant that shock and fluid loss would not be life-threatening, but infection control was vital, as the open, oozing surface of the burns on face, right forearm and upper chest were ideal sites for bacterial infection to take hold.

'We're going to keep you in for a few days,' Drew told the man when he was settled into a bed, with fresh sterile dressings on each wound site, and intravenous fluids flowing through plastic tubing into his uninjured left arm.

'A few days!' Mr Hamilton mumbled, groggy now from the morphine. 'No. . . I've got work to do. . .' But the protest was feeble and soon he had fallen into an uneasy doze.

'Can you really treat him here?' Susan asked with a frown, once she was alone in the reception area with Drew.

'Best to in this case,' he answered. 'He'd hate to be flown to Pendleton, and we're well-equipped to deal with it since it's not over a large surface area.'

'Will he need grafting?'

'No, I very much doubt it. There's no full-thickness burning. Later, once it's all fully healed, his fingers may need some cosmetic surgery to deal with any tightening or webbing of the skin. But we're dealing with the fluid loss and pain. We can handle the higher calorie intake he needs. Infection is the main danger, and the broad-spectrum antibiotics I've used should take care of that. If we could culture a swab from each wound, I'd target the antibiotics more specifically. But in our situation, broad spectrum is better.'

'What else is there to do, then?' Susan asked.

'Routine observations, pain medication. Four-hourly, not on demand, as he's the type who won't ask for it. Dressing changes. We'll do the facial dressing again later tonight, and the others first thing tomorrow. Meanwhile. . .'

'Meanwhile, you get back to Simon,' she told him firmly.

'Do you mind?' She saw how much he wanted to,

and how he was trying to hide it, and felt a painful lurch in her heart. It was all still so hard for him. . .

'Of course I don't mind, Drew. Just bring me some dinner later on.'

'Sure. . .'

He left a few moments later, and she watched him go, aching with an impossible need to touch him, wishing she could just wave some magic wand and make his love for Simon the simple thing it should be. 'Drew. . .' The sound of his name was musical on her lips, escaping without her willing it, then she heard Brian Hamilton calling for her and turned to go to her patient. . .

The sound of hammering echoed off the nearby walls of the gorge and then was overtaken by the more piercing notes of a circular saw. Susan's house was nearly finished. On her way across to the medical centre to open up for a scheduled prenatal clinic, she took a detour over to the building site and noted the changes that had taken place over the past five weeks since she'd arrived there. The roof was finished, and so was the exterior brickwork, but there were no front steps as yet, and no flooring to the veranda. Susan dared to climb a plaster-spattered plank and entered the tiny front hall, to greet the smell of plaster dust and new wood.

The head builder caught sight of her at once and his eyes twinkled as he told her in his strong Scottish accent, 'Another week at the most, I promise you.'

'Jock!' she scolded him lightly. 'You've been saying that for *two* weeks already!'

'I haven't! Well, maybe I have at that, but this time. . .'

'This time I might almost believe you.'

'Will you stay for a cup of tea? It's smoko in a few minutes.' He used the Australian working-man's term for a coffee-break.

'No, I have to open up. We have clinic this morning.'

This time she went through the back door and down another bouncing plank, then cut through an obstacle course of builders' debris to reach the medical centre. As she unlocked its front door, she could see Drew coming down the street from the Arnolds' house, where he had just dropped off Simon.

'Been across to crack the whip over the plasterers, have you?' Drew teased as they met in the waiting-room.

'No need,' she told him. 'The inner walls are going up as fast as the eye can see.'

'Simon will miss your cooking.'

'I'll sell you my recipes.'

'What makes you think they're worth actual money?'

'Oh, I think you'd come round to the same opinion after being pestered often enough for "Cornish pasties like Susan makes".'

'I probably would,' he conceded with a smile.

If Drew's revelation to her about Simon's real parentage had done nothing to further any sensual intimacy between Susan and himself, it certainly seemed to have improved the relationship between him and the child. Drew's secret knowledge, and the pressure it had built in him over three years, was evidently no longer so frightening to the man. The change was a gradual one, as if he was still testing the waters of his feelings, but over four weeks it was clearly perceptible, and was helped enormously by the fact that Simon was now settling in wonderfully well after his very difficult start.

He loved his time at Jane Arnold's each morning, and at Margaret Latham's in the afternoons, and Flora Mowanjum had come to the house several times to baby-sit during minor medical emergencies. She was an aboriginal girl, just out of her teens, and rather shy and soft-spoken after a lifetime lived on the Hamilton family's Namburra Downs cattle station. But she and Simon had already developed a surprising rapport, and

one day the little boy had astonished both Drew and
Susan by coming out with a string of several melodic
syllables 'in Flora's language', as he phrased it—the
local tribal dialect which was still in widespread use.

'It means "I'm hungry",' he told them.

'Did she teach you that?'

'I asked her to. She wanted to teach me "Hello", but
I said I wanted to learn something useful.'

And the dear little thing couldn't understand why
they had both laughed. . .

'Who's on our list for this morning?' Drew wanted
to know now.

'Um, let's see.' Susan checked the appointment book
on the desk. In a minute she would get out each
patient's file. 'Elaine Hamilton, from Namburra
Downs, of course.'

'Good. I'll ask her how Brian is going.'

'He'll need to come in soon, won't he, so you can
assess his need for plastic surgery on that hand?'

'Yes, and, from the way it was healing last week, I
suspect it will,' Drew said. The cattleman had been a
taciturn patient, but his wounds had not developed any
unexpected problems, and he had been discharged,
clearly to his relief, after only three nights.

'Daisy Mowanjum from Namburra Downs, too,'
Susan continued with her list. 'She's married to one of
the stockmen. Also Patsy Strickland, who is the tutor
to the Hamilton children. She's a bit of a ring-in, since
she isn't pregnant at all—she's not married, of course—
but she was due for a check-up and since Mrs Hamilton
and Mrs Mowanjum were both coming in. . .'

'Hmm. It'll be interesting to meet more of the
Namburra Downs contingent. It's meant to be a beautiful property. And that's all?'

'No, Lee Shipton too, actually, for a pregnancy test,
and, she hopes, a first prenatal check-up.'

'Oh! Good news if she is!'

'Yes, she was very happy when she asked for an

appointment the other day. . . And then, first on our list, there are two names I don't recognise. And when I say I don't *recognise* them, I mean I've never *heard* such names before! Ankala and Andara Zebulon, from that tiny little place about fifty kilometres away on the Lawson's River Road. They're not aboriginal names, though, are they?'

'No, I don't think so,' he answered her in an odd tone.

'No, they don't sound it,' she went on in a chatty voice. 'Sound more like space visitors from the star-system Andromeda. Pregnant space visitors. They're both in their eighth month.'

Drew made another non-committal reply and looked across at Susan, who was still studying the appointment book, those innocent eyes in that innocent face arousing in him as usual a reluctant and very surprising degree of physical awareness. He thought back on all the drama of their first week here together—Kylie, the hiker's fall, Simon's mishap of drunkenness—all in such contrast to the four weeks just past which had been so blessedly peaceful.

Simon had badly needed the chance to settle into a reassuring routine, and hadn't asked to ring Kate and Charles in nearly a week now. 'I love you, Daddy,' he had said again last night at bedtime, and for the first time Drew had heard the simple words as a blessing and not as a looming threat, a two-edged sword. His own reply had come more lightly and freely than he would have imagined possible a month ago.

Telling the truth to Susan about Craig and Simon had helped, he was forced to admit, although in the bright light of day the morning after that revelation he had felt regret pounding in him like a nagging tooth-ache. And he couldn't believe that she had shown such wisdom and restraint in the days that followed, not bringing up the issue at all, even in the most indirect way. She had just been friendly, a little reserved for much of the time, occasionally quite cheeky, constantly useful both in her role as a nurse and in her temporary status as his house-mate. She really was a witch of a thing.

And yet. . . He added another item to his mental list of the events which had made that first week such a turmoil. . .their visit to Jambarra Mine and her response to Ted Leighton's venereal disease. A witch of a thing, and so *impossibly* out of touch with the realities of the modern world. If she had been so shocked at Ted Leighton that it had put her off her food, how on earth would she handle Ankala and Andara Zebulon?

He suppressed a sigh as he felt a familiar urge to protect her welling up within him, even while he thought it was time she developed a slightly thicker skin. When it came to the crunch, though, the protective urge won hands down.

Perhaps she needn't know about the Zebulon *ménage*, he decided. After all, she'll only be weighing them and taking their blood-pressure, and so forth. If I could hang on to their charts, which have the personal details. . .

Susan looked up in surprise as Drew took the top two patient history files from the pile she had laid out in front of her.

'I—er—want to look over these,' he mumbled. 'Check them. If you could jot their weight and so forth down on a notepad, I'll enter the figures in their charts later on.'

'Oh, the women with the funny names?' she said. 'Do they have special problems? You got a run-down from the Flying Doctor Service last week, didn't you?'

'Nothing for you to worry about,' Drew said.

'Well, I wasn't worried, but I like to get some background information before——' Too late. He had disappeared into the consulting-room.

The two women arrived minutes later, jolting to a

halt in front of the medical centre in a battered old
station wagon with some very creative patchwork paint.
Four children came with them—one tiny tottering thing
with a runny nose and gummy eyes, dressed in dirty
green overalls, and three slightly older ones, equally
scruffy but with clean faces at least. All of them had
the straw-blonde hair and the freckled, peeling noses
of children who had had constant exposure to the sun.

The waiting-room was soon in a state of chaos.
Hurriedly Susan got out the box of toys and watched
them being scattered to the four corners of the room.
Shrieks of laughter and excitement bounced off the
walls.

They're certainly happy enough, she concluded, in
spite of those scruffy clothes and more than their share
of outback dirt.

In the midst of this chaos, the two heavily pregnant
women moved apparently undisturbed, as if they were
so used to the level of noise and activity that they were
no longer aware of it. They were clearly good friends—
sisters-in-law, perhaps? Susan speculated.

'This is a nice place you've got here,' one said to
Susan.

'We used to have to drive over to Paradoo Station
for the Flying Doctor clinic, but that's an extra forty
kilometres, so this is good,' said the other.

'Yeah, and when Mirabai was born you barely got
back home after the last clinic when you went into
labour, didn't you? The road's that rough up by our
place.'

'The plane hadn't even taken off again from Paradoo
when I'd had the baby! Didn't need the doctor at all by
the time he got there.'

'Well, it was your third. Gets quicker and quicker.'

'Dravadar thought it was a great joke.'

'He did, didn't he?'

They laughed comfortably together. Susan still had
no idea which of them was which, and, with the files

shut up with Drew in his office, she couldn't remember those unusual names anyway.

'I'll start with you, shall I, An. . . Ank. . .?' she began desperately, turning to the woman on the left.

'Fine with me,' she offered cheerfully, not bothering to complete her name on Susan's behalf.

It only took a few minutes to note weight and blood-pressure and test urine, and then the rather pretty brunette was sent in to Dr Kershaw. She emerged again just as Susan had finished taking down the details of the other woman's weight. All in all, it took less than twenty minutes to deal with both patients.

'Dravadar wanted the doctor to have a look at Dalith's eyes if he's got time,' said the fairer of the two women to Susan.

'I think he can manage to fit it in. Has Da. . . Da. . .?' What on earth was that name? She began again. 'Has your little boy had the problem for long?'

'Oh, Dalith's not mine. And she's a girl. We just brought her along because Amintah was feeling a bit queasy today. She thinks she's pregnant too.'

'Oh. OK, well, let's send him. . .*her* in to Dr Kershaw now. One of you had better take good notes of what he says so you can pass it on to Am. . . Amintie,' she hazarded bravely.

'To Amintah. OK, no worries.'

Ten minutes later the two women and four children had left, after all joining in to toss the scattered toys back in the box. Susan looked at the two torn-off pages of her notepad that recorded two sets of blood-pressure and weight readings, each beneath the unhelpful anno-tation of 'A. . .?' She no longer had the slightest idea which figures belonged to which woman.

The group from Namburra Downs was late, and Lee Shipton was scheduled as their last patient of the morning, so Susan took advantage of the lull and went in to Drew to try to deal with her problem. A look at the two charts should provide an adequate clue. One of the women had weighed sixty-nine kilograms and the other seventy-six. Previous prenatal examinations done during Flying Doctor clinic visits should record a regular progression in each woman's weight gain. . .

'Just give me the figures and I'll write them in,' Drew told her.

'No, I'll do it, if you'll give me the chart,' Susan said brightly. She didn't want to confess her dilemma about each patient's identity. It seemed too silly.

'It's no trouble. . .' He held out a hand.

Susan snatched the notepad back. 'Honestly. . .'

Their eyes met and suddenly there was laughter. 'What's going on, Susan?' Drew growled.

'I couldn't work out which woman was which,' she confessed. 'With those names. . .and as for the children. . .! So I need to see the charts to know which one started out heavier, *then* I'll know which figures to put on which chart.'

'Give *me* the figures, for heaven's sake!'

Meekly she handed them over, and watched him note them in. 'Now,' she said. 'if I could have the charts, because I *don't* want to be in this position again! I want to know who is who, which children belong to which, and where the third one fits in who wasn't even *here* today, although one of her children was, because apparently *she's* pregnant now as well! I guess it's three brothers, is it, and their wives? It all seems very eccentric.' She kept holding out her hand but he didn't give her the charts. 'What *is* it, Drew?'

It was quite a stormy exclamation, and her neat little chin was tilted aggressively forward. Her cheeks were growing pink in pretty indignation and he noticed inconsequentially how much better she looked with a touch of outback tan and those golden threads in her brown hair highlighted by sun-bleaching. Contrasting these warm, earthy colours with the positively green tinge her face had taken on three weeks ago after her session with Ted Leighton. . . Surely she would be quite seriously horrified if she knew the truth about Dravadar Zebulon and his *ménage*!

'It's nothing, Susan. Isn't the Namburra Downs crew here yet?'

'No, it's *not* nothing! And no, they're *not* here yet. You've got a look on your face, Drew. . .'

She glowered at him and watched him weaken till finally he said, 'All right. I guess I can't keep it from you. There are three of them—Ankala, Andara and Amintah—and they all regard themselves as the wives of this Dravadar Zebulon. The made-up names are a pretty harmless notion, I think. Six children between them already, and three more on the way, it seems.'

'But their due dates are almost the same!'

'I know. The details are best not thought of, aren't they? I'm sorry, I didn't want to tell you but. . .forgive me, you pestered. And anyway——' suddenly he was impatient as he paced the room. '—you *can't* go on living in your protected shell, Susan! A nurse can't afford to be physically sickened by other people's morals. The women are happy, by all accounts, and they've all been living together for nearly ten years. The children are brought in for medical treatment whenever they're sick, and there are no signs of any neglect or abuse. In fact, they seem very well-loved. As medical people, that's all we can be concerned with. You're not a nun in a cloister. Get off your——'

'Who said I was a nun in a cloister?' she asked him ominously, and watched with satisfaction as he stopped pacing to fling a startled glance across at her. 'And what made you think I'd be physically sickened?'

'Well, you're so innocent. . .' He spread his hands, and the word he had used, coupled with the apologetic tone, only made her angrier.

'Innocent? Yes, I suppose I am. I hadn't realised that made me a less competent member of my profession. Or that it qualified you to treat me like. . . like. . .'

She sputtered into silence, her face burning, and her heart, too. Somehow it was very hurtful that he had tried to protect her in this way. It said so clearly that he regarded her as a creature apart. She remembered his kiss and the way he had called a halt to what was happening. It was part of this same thing now. Misguided. Condescending, beneath its apparent sensitivity.

He was still watching her, perplexed and growing angry now himself. 'Hey, what *is* this?' he said. 'Just try and tell me you *weren't* sickened that day at Jambarra Mine with Ted Leighton!'

'Ted Leighton? That was *completely* different!'

'Why? It was all about sexual morality, wasn't it? Promiscuity?'

'It wasn't at all, although you're right, promiscuity is something I don't personally admire! But I've seen gonorrhoea before. I know that prostitution exists.'

'Then——'

'Of course. . . He didn't do it to you,' she realised. 'Because you're a man. And I was too upset to explain.'

Briefly she sketched the mineworker's behaviour in more detail to Drew—the leering welcome he had given to her professional touch, the deliberately suggestive and very unnecessary detail he had supplied. By the time she had finished, Drew's expression had changed completely.

'My God,' he thundered, 'that's sexual harassment! You could take him to court for that these days.'

'Not really necessary, Drew,' she told him, her own anger ebbing now. 'It was an incident. It's over. Although at the time, yes, I was sickened. I haven't dwelt on it, I promise you.'

'I misjudge you sometimes, don't I?' he said slowly, searching her face. The colour in her cheeks, which had begun to fade, returned.

She nodded, but excused him. 'I expect it's easy enough to do. I admit, the Zebulon family strikes me as weird, no matter how harmless it may be. I'm *not* the most sophisticated person in the world.'

'Pretty sharp, though. . . But that sounds like a four-wheel drive outside. It'll be the Namburra Downs contingent.'

'Nothing in their charts to purse up my prim little mouth, I hope,' she teased.

'Damn! Susan, you don't have a prim little mouth, OK?'

'If you say so.'

'Look! Let's take off for a swim up in Wingoona Gorge this afternoon, shall we? Say half-past one so I can be back to pick up Simon by four? We'll bring the four-wheel drive and stay in radio range.'

'It sounds nice,' she admitted, betraying her pleasure helplessly.

'Then it's settled.'

His smile seemed to shoot into her depths like an arrow, and then—not arrow-like at all—it melted there to leave a warm, creamy feeling of happiness and anticipation. The swim, of course. It would be lovely to spend the afternoon swimming. . .

It was twenty past one. Susan stood in her room, surveying herself and the yellow bathing suit in the full-length mirror on the inside of her wardrobe door. It was utterly ghastly, there was no doubt about that, a left-over from swimming races at school years ago. Once again she mourned the much smarter black and blue Lycra suit and its untimely demise at the hands of laundry bleach.

Four weeks ago at Jambarra Mine, she had laughed it off to Drew and she would just have to do so again. Funny, though, the ugly swimsuit seemed to matter a lot more today, and she almost began to wish she had turned down his invitation. Putting baggy pale khaki shorts and a wide-striped earth-toned T-shirt on top put the problem out of sight for the moment, but. . .

Outside her window, she heard cheerful voices and the banging of car doors. Peeping through the closed curtains, she saw that it was the group of three women from Namburra Downs, and Drew was with them. He had sent Susan off home for lunch as soon as she had done Lee Shipton's pregnancy test—positive!—but hadn't returned to the house for his own meal. He must have gone down to the Shipton's family-style restaurant, and it appeared that the Namburra people had been there too.

Elaine Hamilton took the driver's seat, Daisy Mowanjum was still talking to her sister-in-law Flora, who had walked up with the group from the motel, and Patsy Strickland, tutor to the Hamilton children, was laughing into Drew's face as he told her some amusing anecdote.

Patsy was a very pretty young woman, about twenty-five, with a wild mane of curling strawberry-blonde hair and a tall, rangy figure. She had led an interesting life, too, Susan had gathered this morning, working as a nanny on a yacht that had wandered all over the Pacific Ocean before she had come here to the outback of Western Australia. It certainly looked as if she was taking the change from ocean to desert well in her stride. . .

Susan sat very upright on the edge of her bed and waited. She was ready too early, of course, with hat, sunglasses, sun-block cream and towel already in a canvas bag. She heard Drew enter the house with a bouncing step, and then the door of his room closed smartly. She waited for ten more minutes until he was ready, each minute feeling like five as her mind stewed with a very silly envy of Patsy Strickland. Being ready early gave you too much time to think!

They set off, using the smaller of the medical centre's vehicles and winding along a rough side-track until they came to a parking spot which allowed them to swim within hearing range of the vehicle in case there should be an emergency radio call.

It was a glorious day—quite hot, clear and dry. Laying her towel on the crescent of coarse sand that formed a small beach beside the deep, still reaches of the waterhole, Susan didn't even want to think of swimming. She sat down and leaned back on her hands till she could see all the way up the high walls of the gorge. A hawk circled there, a brown shape against the incredibly blue sky, and she wondered if it was scouting for prey or just enjoying itself as she was, lazily surfing the thermal currents sent up from the warm red rock.

But Drew wasn't feeling lazy today, evidently. He had already flung aside his navy shorts and white T-shirt and was standing at the water's edge. He hesitated for a moment then crashed into the water, letting out a full-bodied yell of exuberance as he reached its colder depths. He swam, using confident efficient strokes to bring himself far out into the sunlit water before turning to splash back to shore again.

'Aren't you coming in?' he demanded, standing ankle-deep and dripping from his water-darkened hair, past his neat black swimming trunks and down to his tightened calves.

'Soon,' she hedged, hugging her arms around her knees.

It was nicer to watch him, and the sun on her back was so delicious. She thought of Melbourne entering its rainy grey winter and shivered. The clear-aired heat of the outback, still strong even now in late April, was new to her and she was beginning to discover that she loved it.

But Drew wasn't going to let her get away with merely stretching out here like a desert lizard soaking up the warmth. 'Hey. . .it's not half as much fun alone, you know.'

And she couldn't say no to him, not when he was standing there like that, so energetic, so unmistakably male, with that cajoling grin on his face. Stripping off shorts and T-shirt, she saw him frown as he glanced at the yellow bathing suit beneath.

'Yes,' she said bright, 'it's me again. The incredible swimming custard. I'm getting a new bathing suit from a catalogue that Margaret lent me, but it hasn't come yet. If the sight of this offends you. . .'

'I don't. . . I didn't. . . Don't apologise.'

'I'm not. Just remember that this very suit won the two hundred metres open backstroke in its last year at school. With me in it, incidentally.'

'Gosh! Did it try out for the state championships?'

'It wanted to, but decided to concentrate on its school work instead.'

He laughed and watched her as she turned her back on him, waded into the water and launched into a neat crawl. He was impressed once again. What business did she have to be reading his expression—or his mind—like that? Ironically, he *hadn't* been frowning at her appearance in the swimming costume this time because, funnily enough, it looked rather nice on her today.

Now, why was that? She had more of a tan now, which formed an attractive honey-gold backdrop to her freckles. Perhaps that was it. Her skin looks like cinnamon toast, he found himself thinking. Very pleasant connotations there. Warm and buttery and sweetly delicious. . .

So was it just the tan that had improved her? Or was it a change in his own perspective? Somehow he was quite uncomfortable with this last idea and pushed it from his mind at once, frowning once again. This was where his thoughts had started, and they were going round in circles.

To break the pattern, he began to think of Patsy Strickland and their conversation over lunch today. She had rather intrigued him. In fact, he had asked her out next weekend on her day off. Not many night-life opportunities in Coolacoola, so he was taking her on a picnic. He told himself that it was Simon who would be in the way at home, but actually it was Susan he kept thinking of.

Thank goodness her house would be finished soon! He didn't expect anything serious to develop between himself and Patsy, but somehow, even if his relationship with Patsy went no further than the odd lunch or dinner, he didn't want it all to happen right under Susan's calm and tactful gaze.

Her gaze. . . She had stopped swimming and was watching him now, the crooked smile on her lips telling him that she was about to make some teasing comment. Forestalling her, he sent an arching splash of water across to drench her shoulders, heard her squeal and laugh, then yelled himself as she returned the drenching in full measure. Seconds later, the skirmish had escalated into a fully fledged battle.

CHAPTER SEVEN

'THERE was a parcel for you in the mail-drop this morning,' Margaret Latham said three weeks later, holding out a brown package to Susan. 'Matt picked up the bag from the airstrip half an hour ago.'

'Thanks, Margaret,' she said. 'It'll be my new bathing suit at last.'

'I guessed as much, and I'm dying of curiosity. Did you pick——?'

'Yes. The red one.' She was opening the parcel as she spoke, and now held up the sleek dark red slip of Lycra by its narrow straps.

'Oh, gorgeous!'

'As long as it fits.'

'I've never had a problem with that catalogue. The sizing always seems about right, and you're so well-proportioned. . . But you're moving today, I hear!'

'Yes, so if you don't mind I won't ask you in,' Susan said apologetically. 'Drew is out all day, and I'd like to be finished by the time he gets back. He's taken Simon over to Namburra Downs.'

'Well, I won't keep you. But don't forget you've got an appointment with Madame Marguerite Hair Design this Friday night at your place, as soon as my baby's asleep!'

'I'll be waiting for you with freshly washed hair and a cake baked in my new oven.'

'Great! We'll have a real girls' night. . .and you can model that bathing suit for me.'

'I will. Thanks again for dropping it round.'

After Margaret had gone, Susan opened the parcel and tried on the dark red Lycra concoction. It did fit, beautifully, and went well with her honey and

117

chocolate-brown colouring. The cut was fashionable
but not too daring, the price had been reasonable, the
quality of the material and workmanship seemed
good. . .and she couldn't care less.

I suppose I'm a bit daunted by the move, she
thought, but this was a pretty weak excuse.

There wasn't all that much to do. The building crew
had moved the furniture in yesterday, and her personal
things could be ferried between here and the new place
in an hour. As for opening all the boxes of kitchen
utensils and linen supplies. . .surely that would be like
an unexpected Christmas in May, even though everything would be fairly plain and serviceable rather than
elegant, designed as it was to serve a succession of
resident nurses down the years.

Another hour of cleaning here at Drew's, because
she wanted to leave the place as nice as she could for
him, and it would all be done. So what was the
problem?

I'm going to miss Simon, she realised, then, allowing
herself to get closer to the truth, And I'm going to miss
Drew.

Idiotic! They'd still be living three doors apart. But
no, it wouldn't be the same. Those small, shared
moments in the kitchen as they cooked or cleared up
together. The sight of his shaving things in the bathroom. The sound of him moving about his room across
the corridor as he undressed at night.

I've enjoyed sharing a place, and now I'll be alone
again, she concluded, not daring to look any further
into the question.

By five-thirty that evening the move was all done,
even down to the arrangement of groceries and perish-
ables in kitchen cupboards and fridge. She and Drew
had divided what was left of Tom Arnold's big shop on
their behalf, and Susan had contracted to go to
Pendleton with Jane in another six weeks to replenish
supplies. For tonight's evening meal tinned soup and

toast would do, she decided, too tired to consider anything else.

Meanwhile, a shower. Emerging from it several minutes later, she went into her new bedroom to dress and saw the four-wheel drive pull up in front of the medical centre just as she finished putting on a denim skirt and cotton knit top. Simon got out first, with a small boy's energy no doubt replenished by a snooze during the drive, then Drew. . .and finally Patsy Strickland. A moment later they had all disappeared into the doctor's house.

Susan gave herself the quiet evening she needed, listening to music on a small tape-deck that she had brought from Melbourne and catching up on letters owed to friends. One other letter as well, which she left until last and tackled reluctantly even then. She should have told her father weeks ago that she had made the move from Melbourne and was living up here.

'Not so far from you any more,' she wrote. '*Only* about twelve hundred kilometres!' In stilted, superficial words, she told him something about her new job and her life, but when the letter was finished and sealed she wondered if any of what she had said would interest him at all.

His life was so removed from hers that there scarcely seemed any connecting points left. He had a pretty wife fifteen years his junior and two equally pretty girls, now in the throes of their Barbie years at eight and ten. He had an airy, opulent house in one of Perth's best suburbs and was absorbed in business interests which she had never known the details of because he had never tried to explain them. . .

Writing to her father always brought on a blue mood. I wonder if he'll reply, she thought. The taped music had switched off and the new house was very quiet. Probably just the usual card in September for my birthday.

She felt claustrophobic and restless, and put on a black wool jacket against the surprising chill of a clear outback night in late autumn, then took the fresh cup of tea she had made and went out to the veranda at the side of the house to sit on the steps. The stars, so bright and vastly distant in the blue-black sky, should soothe her spirits.

There was no moon tonight, and the veranda was very dark. Susan's eyes adjusted slowly until objects resolved themselves out of the night—the shadowy shapes of the river gums, the larger loom of the rocky hills, the faint sheen of the ranger station's galvanised iron roof. It *was* soothing, and restoring, just to observe.

Then she heard the sound of a door closing and quiet voices, and froze where she was as Drew and Patsy came out of his house. She couldn't see them yet. The medical centre building still blocked her view, but when they came round the corner. . .

The governess from Namburra Downs was laughing, and her hair showed off its gorgeous strawberry-blonde hue even in the blue-grey colouring of the night. Drew was laughing too, a low, appreciative cadence of sound that was more like a caress than a laugh. And then he kissed her. Susan saw the two silhouettes meet and blend in the darkness then lowered her gaze to stare stupidly at her own feet, until even these blurred and a silent well of tears overflowed on to her cheeks.

It was vital that she keep silent and still. Absolutely vital. If they realised that she was here, had seen them, was *crying*. . . She saw nothing but the blur of salt water in her eyes and heard nothing but the throbbing of pent-up blood in her ears, and it was a good five minutes before Susan dared to move a muscle. She found a hankerchief in her pocket and pressed it into her eyes, then looked across to where the two figures had been. They were gone now. Back into the house? Down to the motel? She didn't know.

I'm in love with Drew! she realised. How could I have been so stupid? If only I hadn't had to share that house with him for two months!

But she knew that she couldn't lay the blame on this alone. It was so many things—what he had told her about Simon and the way he had told it, the medical dramas they had shared, his body, too. Yes, she couldn't deny that last part. The efficient, muscled forms of his torso and limbs, the red-gold highlights in the brown hair that was often so deliciously untidy, the freckled bridge of his straight nose, the perceptive green eyes, and the firm lips that had kissed her so hungrily just once.

Only once. And now he was kissing someone else, someone far more at home with her own sensuality, someone who had travelled and had seized on life's adventures, someone with a frankly inviting laugh and strawberry-blonde hair that tumbled with deliberate wildness as if to say, Run your hands through this!

Nothing like spinsterish me. And I couldn't be like Patsy Strickland if I tried for a thousand years! Susan told herself.

Rising miserably to her feet, she tossed the rapidly cooling tea out on to the bare red dirt below the veranda steps and hated the desert suddenly. Its landscape was so stark, so uncompromising, with that burnt red rock and earth and those gnarled or spiky or dramatically ephemeral plants and flowers. Somehow the desert made one's own realisations and revelations stark and uncompromising, too——She loved Drew, and she was a fool to do so. Nothing more to it than that.

Restlessly, she entered the house.

Just out of sight down the street, Drew was saying to Patsy Strickland, 'Sorry, I'd walk you back to the motel, only I don't want to leave Simon alone.'

'But you said he never wakes in the night.'

'This would be the one night in a hundred when he did. And even though I'd only be gone ten minutes. . .'

'Actually——' Patsy's voice managed to be both light and throaty '—I was going to ask you in.'

'Oh. . . I see.'

And he did. The invitation was quite frank, and was made even more so when she added, 'But perhaps. . . your place instead?'

'Look, sorry,' he came in reluctantly. 'I'm not the kind of father who's comfortable with the idea of my son waking up unexpectedly to find a woman in my bed.'

'Pity. . .'

'Yes.' Then suddenly he knew that this wasn't the issue at all.

He didn't *want* to bring Patsy Strickland inside his house again and into his bed. Her kiss had been practised in its sensuality, and besides this she was a very interesting young woman. But there was something missing. She was confident, bold, successful, and he found that he was blaming her for this. It took him several seconds to realise why: he was comparing her, and unfavourably too, with Susan. With little Miss Carstairs, whose kiss had been as virginal and tentative as a kiss could be, and yet it had been far harder to resist than Patsy Strickland's hungry mouth. A little bit frightening in its implications, that, but he couldn't think about it now.

'But obviously,' he went on, 'I don't want you walking back to the motel alone in the dark. I have a spare bedroom, and you're more than welcome to——'

She was already shaking her head. 'Skip the gallantry, Drew. I'm quite capable of walking back myself, thanks. It's only a few hundred yards.' She started off as she spoke, her stride long and swinging and confident.

'And you don't need me to drive you back to Namburra Downs tomorrow?' He couldn't wait now for this scene to end.

'No. Mr Hamilton is coming in anyway,' she answered easily.

'That's right. I'm taking a look at his burns.'

'Goodnight, then, Drew.'

'Night, Patsy.' He breathed a sigh of relief as he watched her walk away. He turned to walk back into the house. But by the time he had reached his front door he had forgotten about Patsy. Susan Carstairs was the subject that was gnawing at his mind, and suddenly she had become something that needed a lot of thought. . .

'What do you think?' Margaret Latham hovered anxiously behind Susan as she studied her reflection in the brightly lit mirror of her new bathroom. There she saw a fresh haircut that showed off a long neck and hid a forehead that was a little too square.

'Well. . . It's scary,' she said.

'Scary?'

'Yes. New. Me, but new.'

'You like it?'

'I love it, and that's what's scary. I've never loved the way I look before.'

She gave an almost apologetic smile, and Margaret shook her head. 'Funny girl. You don't seem quite sure.'

'Oh, I am!' She tossed her head and felt the lightness of it, the way the hair fell so cleanly around her face, and the cool of the breeze on her neck. 'And it *will* be nice and cool.' Silly thing to say. Better, though, than saying, And Drew will like it, which was what she was thinking deep inside. She changed the subject quickly. 'Let's go and have coffee and cake.'

'Mm, so you really did make one?'

'Of course. I said I would.'

'What kind?'

'My ingredients were slightly limited. Chocolate and vanilla marble cake with chocolate and orange icing.'

'Ooohh!'

'And Rose Portland brought me a big tub of choc-
olate-chip ice-cream when the Flying Doctor plane
dropped in here on Wednesday.'

'Ice-cream?' Margaret moaned. 'We haven't had that
in the house for two months. Didn't it melt on the
plane?'

'A bit,' Susan admitted. 'Though she packed it in a
cooler with ice. But it refroze in my new fridge.'

'Don't expect to get rid of me for at least an hour,
then. I'm going to gorge.'

'You deserve to.' Susan tossed her head again and
laughed. It felt wonderful.

'Tell that to my fat cells! They're just panting to fill
up to bursting point.'

'Well, you have your "secret weapon", don't you?'
Susan said lightly. Actually, it was a probe. That phrase
of Margaret's had stuck with her over the past seven
weeks and she was still faintly suspicious of it. A couple
of times, she had almost gone to Margaret's file, kept
alphabetically under 'L' for Latham in their efficient
filing system at the medical centre. Perhaps she would
find some clue there. But this was where the line
between personal and professional became awkwardly
blurred, and in the end she hadn't done it. It would
have felt like snooping. But now. . .

'Oh, yes. My secret weapon. . .' The other woman
had coloured a little. 'It's nothing, really. It's not that
I do anything silly. It's just a way of putting my system
in balance, when you look at it. Anyway. . .' She
flapped her hand, dismissing the subject, and Susan's
curiosity and concern were heightened.

She *is* doing something she shouldn't. But what, I
wonder? Surely she's not bulimic? she thought.

The small mystery took the edge off Susan's pleasure
as she prepared their coffee and produced the cake,
and it was only Margaret's moans of ecstasy and shrieks

of disbelief at the sight of the latter that distracted her from the subject.

'Suu-saan Car-stairs! You did this yourself? It's stunning. Those chocolate rosettes! And that bow around the side, that's made of orange icing, isn't it? It could be in some swanky French patisserie.'

'Well, it's more German in style, but yes.'

'That icing looks like the kind that wins prizes at shows.'

'I did win a couple of third prizes in Melbourne,' Susan admitted. She had taken a lot of trouble over the cake and was glad to have it appreciated, both because she wanted to repay all Margaret's work with sewing machine, scissors and combs, and because it was, along with her embroidery, a creative outlet that she thoroughly enjoyed.

'Oh, did you?' Margaret was saying. 'And why hasn't Coolacoola seen this side of you before?'

'I didn't have my own kitchen and I didn't want to bother Drew with my fussing around and mess-making.'

'Oh, yes!' Margaret said sarcastically. 'I'd be very bothered by someone concocting this sort of thing. But who taught you?'

'My aunt. Aunty Dot.'

'The one who brought you up and taught you that exquisite needlework as well?'

'Yes.'

'Very maidenly pursuits. Cake-baking and decorating, and fine needlework.'

'Very maidenly,' Susan agreed cheerfully.

'Hmm.' Margaret narrowed her eyes suspiciously. 'The real reason why you didn't make anything like this for Drew? Didn't want him to think you were trying to ensnare him with domesticity?'

'I—ensnare? What do you mean?'

'Come, come, child! He's available and very eligible. Don't you have just the tiniest bit of a——'

'No! Absolutely not!' Susan marshalled her rather meagre reserves of deceitfulness and added quickly, 'I'd *never* be interested in a man who. . .who'd already been married and had a child.'

'Oh, you wouldn't?'

'No.' Susan didn't care if it made her sound narrow-minded, and didn't try to explain any further.

'I suppose it could be difficult. . .' Margaret responded.

Susan didn't know if she was really convinced, but it would be worse to harp on the subject. What was that line about protesting too much? She said instead, stoutly and this time truthfully, 'In any case, I doubt that he's looking for anything serious.'

This time she could see that Margaret truly agreed. 'No, probably not. He's been seeing a bit of Patsy Strickland, I know. . .'

'Yes. A far better prospect, don't you think?'

'We'll have to find someone else for you, then. All this blossoming you've been doing can't be allowed to go to waste.'

'Blossoming?' The colour on her cheeks was certainly blossoming.

'Yes.'

'Oh, rubbish!' Though she had felt it herself, not trusting it, wondering if any of it showed. . .particularly to Drew.

'A very rapid one. Jane has said so too, more poetically than me—"like flowers in the desert after rain".'

'Please, Margaret. . .'

'Love——' a hand, glinting with fashionable rings, settled on her shoulder for a moment '—I'm not teasing. I'm just saying go for it, whether "it" is Drew, or someone else, or just *life*.'

'Well, I'm trying,' she admitted. 'For life, that is.' Then, too flustered to stand the subject of either Drew or herself a moment longer, she said, 'Now, stop chattering and let's cut this cake, for heaven's sake!'

'You do it. . .and make it a big fat slice for me, please!'

A big fat slice. Margaret had ended up eating three, with a relish that satisfied the cook in Susan but worried the nurse in her more than a little. Now, nearly a week later, the picture was still vivid—well-groomed Margaret licking her fingers and taking big bites like a greedy child, all with a smugness and relish that suggested she *did* have something to 'neutralise the calorie bombs'. Or she thought she did.

Thumbing through the files to prepare for a morning of routine appointments, Susan came across 'Latham, Margaret' and paused, her fingers resting on the top of the rows of manila.

'Is Margaret due for a check-up soon?' she asked Drew, who had just been on the phone to the health department in Perth and was now drinking his morning coffee.

'No idea. Why?' he asked.

'Probably nothing.'

'But maybe something. Tell me about it.' Susan told her meagre story and he shrugged. 'Diet pills, do you think?'

'No, nothing as straightforward as that.'

'She hasn't needed any medical treatment since we've been here. I'm not even sure if she has any health problems or unusual medical history. Look through her chart. There may be a clue.'

'I will. If I have time before——'

She broke off. The door to the centre had just opened to admit Ted Leighton. It was his file she had been looking for when she had come across Margaret's. Here it was, straight after 'Latham'. Drew quickly took his coffee and the pile of patient files from Susan's hand and retreated to his consulting-room.

'He'll be ready for you in a minute,' Susan told the man from Jambarra Mine.

'I don't mind waiting, darling,' he leered, lunging close to her so that she was aware of his sour breath. But she gritted her teeth. She was prepared this time, and he *wasn't* going to get to her.

'Oh. You'd like to catch up on some reading, would you?' She picked up a large pile of magazines and dumped them into his arms with a brittle smile.

He grunted at the impact and she retreated quickly behind the desk, found some large scissors in the top drawer and began the completely unnecessary task of cutting scrap paper into memo-sized pieces. Her strategy paid off. Mr Leighton had put down the magazines and ambled over to her once again. 'Got any coffee for the patients?'

'If you like, yes.'

'I've got the runs. . .or the back door trots, as my Grandad used to call 'em.'

'So did mine.'

'Can't seem to get rid of it, you see. That's why I've come.'

'Well, do feel free to use the back door, if you like, although we do have a nice patients' bathroom just along the corridor there.' She pointed with the scissors, brandishing them very freely so that the man was forced to retreat from his cosy snuggle over the top of her desk.

'But do you think coffee'll make it worse, Nurse?' he asked.

'Try it and see. Coffee supplies are in the corner *there*. Milk is in the fridge just *there*. Help yourself.' Another wild brandishing of the scissors. This time he almost had to duck, and as he slunk away she saw Drew standing in the doorway of his consulting-room, fighting to suppress a laugh.

'I'll see the—er—patient now,' he managed.

'You can go in, Mr Leighton,' Susan told the mineworker unnecessarily, approaching him with scissors in hand like a cattle prod. He ducked them in alarm, and almost scuttled through the consulting-room door ahead of the doctor.

Drew turned and gave Susan a hearty thumbs-up sigh, murmuring, 'Ten points for initiative and improvisation.'

'Improvisation! I've had these scissors at the ready for weeks!' And she was so pleased with herself that she forgot to look at Margaret Latham's file as she had planned to do.

It wasn't until Ted Leighton was long gone and the appointment list had no more names left on it that Susan thought about Margaret again. And that was only because she walked into the centre, cheerful and energetic as ever, with fresh blonde steaks in her hair, just as Drew was ushering out a talkative elderly patient from the tiny town of Hall's Junction forty kilometres away.

'Hello, Margaret,' Susan said. 'You're not on our list this morning. Does that mean the new catalogue you wanted to show me came on the mail plane?'

'No, it didn't.' Margaret made a face. 'It's late this month. No. . .' She laughed. 'Silly me, though. I accidentally knocked my bottle of thyroid pills off the bathroom shelf yesterday and it shattered. I couldn't pick the pills out of the glass so I threw them away and I need some more.'

'Thyroid pills?' Drew asked, watching her from across the room.

'Yes. I probably haven't even mentioned it. Dr Greeley did my last check-up before the Flying Doctor Service handed over to you, so I haven't needed to see you yet. I had Graves's disease several years ago and they zapped my thyroid a bit too much. Now I have to take replacement thyroxine.'

'So you'll need a new lot?' Drew asked.

'Yes, please.'

'How many were left in the old bottle?'

'Oh—er—gosh, I can't remember.' She seemed a little flustered and something suddenly clicked into place in Susan's mind. Her eyes met Drew's across the room and she saw he had had the same idea.

'We're in the middle of reorganising the dispensary, Margaret,' she came in quickly and untruthfully. 'I'm not sure where I'd find our thyroxine at the moment. Can you come back this afternoon, after pre-school?'

'Oh, no problem,' Margaret said. 'But I did miss yesterday's dose, so——'

'Actually, why don't I just drop them round at your place?' Susan suggested, and a minute later the other woman had gone.

'Her "secret weapon"?' Drew asked at once. 'Could it be?'

'It's what I'm wondering. But *thyroxine*?'

'I know. Dangerous and inefficient as a weight loss method.'

'But, yes, much as I like Margaret, she's the kind of person that might think along those lines.'

'Too little thyroid function makes you fat, and too much makes you thin. Thyroxine replaces thyroid function, therefore an extra pill here and there. . .'

'Will help keep the weight off.'

'Hell, I'd better sit her down and help her get rid of that idea.'

'Then you think I'm right?'

'It fits the facts, doesn't it? Good detective work, Susan. So she didn't really break a half-full bottle of pills.'

'No, she'd taken extra ones along the line and she's run out ahead of schedule.'

'Go out and call her back. She can't have gone far. . . No, on second thoughts, I'll race and catch up with her. She's probably going straight back to Jane's, and I have to pick up Simon for lunch.'

'Yes, better to make it an informal talk. Less threatening that way.'

'But I'll *be* threatening if I have to. Lock up here, will you?'

'Of course.'

'And Susan?'

'Yes?' He was smiling, his green eyes softened in a way that made her insides turn upside-down.

'You're really thinking on your feet these days. I. . . enjoy working with you, and we make a good team.'

'Oh. Thanks,' she answered clumsily, and he had gone before she could regain the poise that still felt so new and shaky at times. Nice to hear some praise like that. Silly to wish it had been more personal, less professional. . .'

The centre was closed that afternoon, and Susan had planned to swim. Yes, she admitted to herself—she hoped that Drew might turn up at the waterhole as well. He liked to take Simon out of his little pre-school sometimes, to make up for the times when he was called out at odd hours. He liked to swim alone too. Several times she had seen him setting off with a towel slung over his shoulder. And twice he had invited Susan along. Golden times in her memory, too vivid, too important.

It's just swimming, she told herself today as she packed a bag with book, sunscreen, hat and snack. It's not even as if we've talked much at the waterhole, let alone touched. . .

And in the end she couldn't go.

'Call from Lawson's River,' Drew told her, appearing at the door just as she was about to set off. 'Ankala Zebulon is in labour, and, if it's anything like her last, we'd better get there quickly.'

'I've got my swimming costume on.'

'Leave it,' he teased. 'They may have a pool and you can grab a swim once it's all over.'

'A pool? What, marble and fifty feet long? But tell me about your talk with Margaret. . .'

'She's very chastened, realises how silly it was, says to thank you for catching her out. And I've convinced her that her weight to height ratio is just about perfect already. I'll tell you our conversation in more detail as we drive, if you like.'

'Do, because I *do* like Margaret.'

They were on their way at once, and Drew stormed along the dirt road that led to Lawson's River, sending out billows of dust like a jet trail. The vehicle vibrated in harsh rhythm with the corrugations, and he had to grip the wheel tightly to keep control. It was extremely noisy, too, and Susan had to ask him to repeat himself several times.

'Outback veterans say that the faster you drive on these corrugations, the less they vibrate,' he shouted to her at last. 'Shall I test the theory?'

'I think you're testing it already,' Susan shouted back as the speedometer crept over the hundred k.p.h. mark.

'Is that a hint that you'd like me to slow down?'

'Yes!'

He laughed, and the rhythm of the jolting eased. The journey took only half an hour, and when they arrived at the odd collection of buildings that was Dravadar Zebulon's property they hurried inside.

In a bedroom draped with Indonesian batik cloth and smelling of patchouli oil Ankala Zebulon lay, being ministered to by a woman who must be Amintah, the third of Dravadar's 'wives'. They both smiled apologetically. 'Too late, again . . .' Drew said.

Amintah held out a bundle of swaddling. 'Fifteen minutes ago. Isn't he beautiful?'

'He is,' Drew said, taking the child. 'And let's make sure he's healthy as well.'

'Sure cried enough.'

'Susan, why don't you check the baby, while I look at Ankala and make sure the placenta is fully expelled?'

'He's a darling. Where can I examine him?' Susan said to Amintah.

'Here. Lay him on this sheet. We boiled some linen in the copper last week so it would be really clean. And here. . . You too, Doctor, if you want to wash your hands. . .'

'Thanks.' A door led from the bedroom to the veranda, where a basin fed by a large old toilet cistern was fixed to the wall in the open air. Drew took his turn first, then Susan.

Then she examined the baby for heart-rate, respiratory effort, muscle tone and other signs, measured his head circumference and weighed him on the kitchen scales that Amintah produced. He looked alert and robust, wearing nothing but a thin cloth nappy. She was taking that off too, just as Drew came over. 'The placenta is intact and she didn't tear. Now, the baby. . .'

'He's healthy and——' Susan stopped. They both saw it at once as she took off the nappy. A small abnormality, relatively common.

'Hypospadias. . .' Drew examined the tiny organ carefully.

'What? What's wrong' The newly delivered mother stirred and tried to sit up, sensitive to every nuance of tone when the subject was her baby.

'Your little boy has a slight problem with his penis,' Drew explained. 'The urethra isn't quite where it should be. From what I can see, this looks like a very mild version. It's called hypospadias.'

'He won't be ill or infertile, or. . .?'

'No, nothing like that. Please don't worry. When he's seven or eight months old, we'll pop him into hospital in Perth for some very minor surgery. He'll be in for one night at the most.'

'Oh, good!' Both women were relieved.

Amintah caressed the tiny face, now scrunched up in sleep, and Susan found herself thinking that if a man had three wives, then his children probably didn't suffer from having three mothers. There was certainly a lot of love in this odd household.

'I wish Zeb was here. . .' Ankala was saying. 'But I'd better break it to him gently. Men are so weird about that bit of anatomy!'

Then they all heard a car. 'That might be him now,' Amintah said, then explained to Drew and Susan, 'He's been up at his mine today, running the crusher. Got two ounces of gold from it this past six months.'

But it wasn't Dravadar Zebulon who had pulled up outside. It was Brian Hamilton. He raised his eyebrows when he heard about the new baby, still less than an hour old. 'Came to pick up a chain-saw that Zeb's been fixing for me. He's a wizard at that stuff. Odd bloke, though. . .'

'Chain-saw's in the red shed. It's fixed,' said one of the children, a boy of about seven. 'I'll show you.' The two of them went off together, leaving Drew and Susan standing awkwardly.

'I'd like to meet the man,' Drew said. 'Look at all this. . .'

There actually *was* a pool. Andara Zebulon was supervising the children as they splashed in it—an old water-tank that had a wooden deck added around it and marine life painted in weird and wonderful colours all over inside and outside. An old car body had been likewise spruced up and filled with earth, now serving as a flower-box for rioting nasturtiums in red, orange and yellow.

A rain-water tank up on a tall stand dripped from several holes so that the ground beneath was moist, and tomatoes, peppers and beans grew there. Three old houses, clearly hauled here from other sites, were now connected by screened walkways, and the superficial impression of chaos and untidiness dropped away on closer examination to reveal ingenuity and care in the way each run-down object had been given a new lease of life in a surprising role.

'Mr Hamilton can be pretty sure his chain-saw is fixed, I think,' Susan commented, and at that moment the sound of it roared from the shed, which was indeed painted a very vivid red. A moment later, the owner of Namburra Downs emerged.

'Good as new,' he said, lugging it in his right hand. Then he gave an irritated grimace and shifted the heavy machine to his left. 'Damn this hand!'

'Let's have a look,' Drew said.

'You've seen it, Doc,' Brian Hamilton growled. 'The skin's all tight, and no, I'm *not* letting some gimcrack plastic surgeon in Perth get hold of it! I'll just have to get used to it!'

'It's your decision. . .' the doctor answered neutrally.

Susan knew that he had tried to persuade Mr Hamilton to have surgery before this, but the outback-bred cattleman was too suspicious, too stoical, too stubborn. He took the chain-saw and counted some money into Andara Zebulon's hand. 'Zeb said twenty dollars, but here's thirty. She hasn't purred like this since I bought her.'

'Thanks, Mr Hamilton.'

He laid the machine in the back of the station vehicle and had soon driven away, at a speed which prompted Susan to say, 'I see he subscribes to the theory about going faster to dampen the vibrations.'

'We'd better get going too,' Drew said to Andara. 'I'll be back tomorrow to check on things, and of course you'll radio the centre if you have any questions or problems at all.'

'Oh, don't go,' Andara said. 'Have a swim, maybe.' She gestured at the water-tank.

'Well. . .'

'Or a cup of tea. I made a carrot cake this morning. . .'

'No, I think——'

'Doctor, I think you'd better stay.' This time it was rather more urgent. 'You see, Ankala seems to have set me off too. I've been having contractions for the past hour. . .'

This one took longer. At first things were quite easy and Drew and Susan did have their swim, the former using as swimming trunks a pair of khaki shorts he had in the vehicle. The tank pool was filled with bore-water and it was a little too harsh and warm to be refreshing. More like a health spa, with all those mineral salts, Susan decided.

There was time for tea and carrot cake, too, but then there was work to be done, moving Ankala and her baby to another room and preparing the largest bedroom for Andara. Dravadar Zebulon came back from 'his mine', and Susan was a little disappointed to find him a rather ordinary-looking man, tubby about the middle and fully bearded. He helped Amintah with the children, while Ankala and her tiny boy slept.

Andara's contractions were increasing now in intensity, frequency and duration.

'Eight centimetres dilated. It won't be long now,' Drew told Susan. But it was dark outside already, and he had arranged by radio for Simon to stay late at Margaret's and spend the evening with Flora.

'Help! I can't! I forgot it was this awful,' the labouring woman moaned as a fresh contraction gripped her.

'Only a few more now,' Drew said. 'You're doing well. Keep up your breathing. You're in control.'

He took both her hands in his and forced her to meet his steady gaze, then joined in the breathing with her until the ragged, panicky rhythm had steadied and she rode out the pain more comfortably. He stayed with her constantly after this, and Susan watched. He was so good at it.

Then she remembered. Of course! He had been at Simon's birth. He knew, as much as any man could, how the minutes passed with such feverish slowness as you breathed through every contraction. Poor Drew! She felt a twisting pain of empathy for him suddenly, understanding more completely now how his memories must hurt and torture him. Lisa, labouring, taking all Drews's love and help, to give birth to another man's son, and keeping her secret for fourteen more months after the birth. If he never trusted a woman again, never wanted another child in his life, could she blame him?

Perhaps it would be better if what I'd said to Margaret about him were true, Susan thought miserably. If I really *didn't* want to have anything to do with a man who'd been married before. . .

'Fully dilated,' he reported ten minutes later. 'She'll need to push any minute now.'

And, as if on cue, Andara Zebulon began to strain and tremble, panting heavily to regain her breath between each merciless contraction. The baby's head, dark with hair, crowned and stretched the open cervix. Susan braced herself against one foot and Drew against the other as Andara pushed and the head began to emerge.

'Stop, Andara, stop if you can,' Drew urgerd her suddenly. 'Pant. Like this—h-h-h-h. You're tearing.'

With sharp efficiency he prepared a local anaesthetic, injected it into her perineal area then made a small cut, which would heal far more neatly than a jagged tear. A minute later the head was out, and he carefully rotated the shoulders, easing them through on the next contraction.

'Ahh!'

'She's born, Andara. She's here!' Susan said.

'A beautiful girl,' Drew came in. 'Look!'

'Call Zeb. Call Zeb.' She was panting and laughing and crying all at once. 'He gets too jittery beforehand but he'll want to see her straight away. We're going to call her Nairee.'

It was late when they took the road back to Coolacoola, and this time Susan was at the wheel. Stretching his shoulders in the passenger seat, Drew said, 'It's been a good day, Susan.'

'It has. . .' Funny, she was tired, but it was a very satisfying tiredness.

'We convinced Margaret Latham to find a more reasonable form of weight loss. We delivered one baby and made sure another one got here safely. Brian Hamilton is still being stubborn as hell about his hand. . .'

'Perhaps, as he says, he'll get used to it.'

'He'll have to, if he won't have surgery. But do you know what the best bit was?'

'What? Our swim in that marble swimming-pool?'

'No. The sight of you keeping Ted Leighton at bay with those scissors.'

And they laughed—comfortably, like friends—as Susan made the turn-off on to the main road to Coolacoola.

CHAPTER EIGHT

'You're early,' Susan told Drew one Wednesday night about two months later. 'And where's Simon?'

She had invited the two of them over to dinner, one of several such invitations that had gone both ways between them. Nice. Friendly. Nothing more. Susan had started to feel quite pleased with herself for schooling her emotions so that friendship was satisfying enough.

'I'm not here for dinner, Susan,' he told her. 'There are four hikers missing up in the Birradindi Creek section of the park and Tom Arnold wants our help.'

'Birradindi Creek! But that's a heck of a drive, isn't it?'

'Four hours, Tom reckons, and he wants us to head off as soon as possible so we can start the search and rescue at first light. Flora will be coming to mind Simon in half an hour. Meanwhile——'

'We can eat the casserole straight away.'

'Good girl. And I'm bringing a Thermos. Get the kettle on and pack up some tea and coffee supplies. Jane and Margaret are making sandwiches and cutting cake, as well as putting together the makings of several more camp-style meals.'

'My goodness, is this a rescue or a banquet?'

'Susan, it's a very isolated area and there are four people missing. We may be gone for a couple of days. . .'

It was thoroughly dark already and growing colder when they left half an hour later. July was the heart of the short desert winter, and though the days were still warm—almost hot in the direct sun—the nights cooled rapidly and could even produce a frost.

'Fill me in, Drew,' Susan said to Drew as she took the first stretch at the wheel.

'There are four of them, as I told you,' Drew said. 'An older man, two of his sons, and the older son's wife. They were well-equipped and had a clear itinerary planned. They've been out for three nights already, and were due back at the camping ground today. When the hiking party hadn't returned by dark, the non-hikers in the family went to Tom and raised the alarm.'

'So if there's been some accident, or if they're lost, it could have happened three days ago.'

'Exactly. It adds an edge of urgency, as does the fact that they picked the most inaccessible part of the park. Tom says that bringing in a helicopter to help in the search and rescue would be risky and he's very anxious to avoid that option if we can.'

'Those three men who are driving with Tom and Matt. . .'

'The daughter's husband, and two volunteers who had made friends with them at the camping ground. Tom will radio for more help if we haven't found them by Friday morning, I imagine.'

'We have a map of their planned route, and where they intended to leave their vehicle?'

'Yes. And it could be something as simple as car trouble. They don't have two-way radios in the vehicle.'

As they drove, Susan's world narrowed to the dark shape and wildly swimming beam of headlights in front of her that was Tom and Matt's vehicle. Then Drew took his turn and they made crazy conversation just to keep him awake and alert. By the time they arrived, it was nearly midnight. The missing hikers' vehicle stood in the expected place, driven off the rough track to a camp-spot down beneath some trees that lined the dry bed of Birradindi Creek.

'Vehicle's not locked and keys are in the ignition,' Tom said. 'I'm going to start it and drive it a half-mile or so. That way, we'll know for sure they didn't have engine trouble and try to walk somewhere for help.' They all watched as he put the vehicle through its paces. No problem, apparently.

Meanwhile, Matt had lit a fire. 'We'll keep this going all night,' he said. 'They might see it. So if people could collect some wood. . .'

Once a large woodpile had been made, they all ate sandwiches and drank tea from the Thermos, thankful for warmth and refreshment as they stood around the fire to keep the chill at bay. Then it was time to sleep. There were three tents, two catering for two people and the third for three. Seven people altogether—six men, and Susan. Drew had made the same calculation. 'Take the tent,' he told her in a gruff undertone. 'I'll take the back seat of the vehicle.'

'OK.' There was no point in arguing, as she saw at once that he had made up his mind. Matt built up the fire, surrounding it with heavy river stones to keep it well-contained. He or Tom would check it during the night. A few minutes later everyone had retired into their tents.

Susan didn't sleep well. The sleeping-bag was warm but the ground, beneath only a thin sheet of dense foam rubber, was hard and her bundled-up spare clothing made an inadequate pillow. When Tom called to her and batted the nylon roof of the tent to awaken her before six the next morning, she was stiff and aching. Struggling into her clothes, she found outside that dawn was still a long way off and the air was chilly and damp with dew. Only a faint pale glow on the eastern horizon promised that the sun would ever rise again at all.

Suddenly, Drew was beside her. 'Here,' he said. 'Wash your face with this. It'll refresh you.'

She took the towel he held out and found that one corner of it was wet with the last of the hot water from the Thermos. He was right. It *did* feel good on her face. After using the dry half to buff her skin as well, Susan was able to look around and see that the camp, improvised so quickly in last night's darkness, was already busy and the fire built up.

Over a hearty breakfast of eggs, bacon and toast they discussed the plan for the day. The men would fan out in three teams of two, each taking a different area of terrain which Tom Arnold outlined clearly on the map. There were three portable radios, one for each team, but only Tom's could communicate with the more powerful radio units in the two vehicles. Hourly call-ins were arranged. The teams were decided on— Tom and Peter, Matt and Graham, Drew and Alan.

'And what about me?' Susan said quietly. 'Who do I go with?'

'You stay here,' Tom said.

She nodded, not surprised at the decision, then caught Drew's quickly bitten-off, 'But——'

'That's fine,' she said. 'I'll work the radio, report back to the Flying Doctor Service. . .and keep the kettle on!'

'That's the idea,' Tom laughed. 'But seriously. . . keep a good smoking fire today, lots of leaves and green branches. They're more likely to see a plume of smoke than a night-time blaze. And give the car horn a good steady beep every half-hour.'

'Every half-hour,' Susan nodded.

'Tom, shouldn't someone else stay? Susan will be alone!' Drew burst out at last. He had gone along with all the plans until now. He liked Tom Arnold, and the frequent contact they had was generating a solid friendship. Susan herself looked quite calm about the idea, too, and hadn't tossed a grateful glance in his direction as he had half expected her to do, but. . .

'Whoever stays will have to stay alone,' Tom said.

'If you're afraid that Susan's not fit enough for a long hike, she is,' Drew insisted. He was drawing attention to himself with his protesting, wasting precious time

too, but couldn't help himself. This place was so lonely
that the missing hikers hadn't even bothered to take
the keys out of their car. . .

'You don't mind, do you, Susan?' The head ranger
turned to her, and she shook her head easily, her bell
of brown hair catching the first rays of the morning sun
and taking on a hue of burnt gold.

Drew was angry with her. A little feminine helplessness would have been nice! Didn't she realise how
alone she was going to be? She did, he saw, and she
was—as usual!—taking it quietly in her stride. She still
hadn't looked at him.

'Good!' Tom Arnold was saying, as if that simple
shake of the head settled the matter. 'Because the men
are stronger if we need to carry anyone out. . .and we
need your experience with the radio.'

The matter *was* settled, Drew realised, and only now
did he begin to question his reponse to the issue. He
wasn't usually the chivalrous type. Damn her! She was
doing it to him again! Laying siege to all his certainties
about himself without even trying. They had been at
Coolacoola for over four months now, and every time
he kidded himself that he had her safely pigeon-holed
in the category of 'good friend and colleague' something like this happened and he caught himself behav-
ing in a way that seemed quite out of character. . .

Rousing himself, he focused on the plans for the
search once more. An hour later, the three teams were
ready to depart, each equipped for an overnight camp-
out, should it prove necessary. A site had been decided
on for a makeshift airstrip, too, and Susan would spend
the time between her half-hourly horn-tooting and
radio stand-bys in marking the strip as clearly as
possible and removing as much debris from the site as
she could. For her more than anyone it would be a
long day.

Watching her, Drew saw that she still seemed quite
calm and prepared. How could I ever have thought her

plain? he wondered inappropriately. The short bob
that Margaret Latham had given her had done something to her face. That lightly tanned neck looked even
longer and more graceful now, and the golden net of
threads on the top of her head got lighter and more
golden every day in the sun.

Today she wore baggy jodhpur-style trousers, and
probably didn't realise quite what delicious things the
cut of them did to her compactly curved rear end. The
sleeves of a dark blue wool pullover were casually
rolled to her elbows, and the tiny frown tucked
between her brows spoke of a preoccupation with the
business of the day that made him itch to shatter it with
some attention-commanding gesture. Totally out of
line!

Tom was going over their plans one last time and
giving a short, laconic pep-talk in typical Australian
outback style. Drew hadn't heard a word of it. Tom,
Peter, Matt and Graham shouldered their packs and
set off in a foursome, as their route was shared for the
first half-mile or so. Alan had disappeared discreetly
down the creek for a few minutes. Out here there were
no bathrooms, of course. So Drew and Susan were
temporarily alone, standing around a fire which
smoked horribly.

He opened his mouth to say, Let's move away, but
she got in first, and for the first time he realised that
she was angry with him, and must have been so all
morning.

'Drew, did you have to say in front of everyone that
you didn't think I should be the one to stay here
alone?' Her voice was very low and very vibrant. 'I
hadn't realised that you thought I was incompetent.'

'Incompetent? I don't——'

'Then why? What was the problem? I was
embarrassed!'

'The problem? Damn it!' Suddenly she was in his
arms, and he knew he had pulled her there, but it

hadn't been a planned action at all. '*I'm* the problem! I was worried about you! I still am!' He bent and kissed away her reply, so that her words became just sounds — first as she fought his kiss then as she responded and drank it in. 'Oh, Susan!'

'Drew. . .'

He smelt of the outback, that odd combination of freshness and dust, sweat and eucalyptus that she could never make up her mind about. It should have been unpleasant, shouldn't it? Yet definitely it was anything but. Her anger against him evaporated as quickly as the desert dew, and her arms locked tightly around him as she parted her lips to taste him as completely as she could.

Already she was melting, throbbing inside, and wanting so much more than just this moment. The light desert breeze gave a fillip of movement that threw a cloud of pungent smoke from the fire all over them, and she felt her eyes stinging and her nostrils filling with a dry, acrid sensation. Not the place or the time for a kiss at all. And yet she couldn't bear for it to stop. His hard thighs pressed against her and she arched her back, wanting to feel his muscled chest against the soft, tingling cushions of her breasts. His hands were in her hair and making soft, feather-light strokes on her bare neck.

But it was time for Drew to leave, as they could hear Alan on his way back.

'You'll radio to Tom on the hour?' Drew reminded Susan unnecessarily.

'Mm-hmm.'

'Take care. . .' The two simple syllables seemed to catch in his throat and he ran the warm palm of his hand lightly along her jawline, then he turned and headed off with Alan to cross the dry creek-bed.

'Why did he have to do that?' Susan scolded impotently aloud to the empty camp.

Until his kiss, she *hadn't* minded too much about the

prospect of loneliness today. Now, suddenly, she did, and it was all Drew's fault. What a time to kiss her! Just like a soldier going off to war and leaving a woman to wait behind, breaking her heart in uncertainty and confusion. Kissed and left behind. Kissed and forgotten.

Well, I can be a soldier too! she told herself as she walked steadily up to the airstrip site to begin her task. I've got plenty to do!

Clearing the airstrip was hot, slow and tiring work, and the break that came for ten minutes in each half-hour when she returned to camp to man the radio and stoke the fire was a very welcome one. By half-past four, she had finished the task. Back at camp, exhausted, she simply sat on a comfortable log for a long time, stoking the bed of ashes and coals and staring at the licking of flames and the sinuous curling of smoke.

Then she realised that it was getting dark. . .

'Going OK, Susan?' A radio call from Tom at six o'clock.

'I'm fine.' But she had to put more effort into the words now. The sun had dropped behind the rocky walls to the west and the sounds of the outback evening had taken on a more mysterious note. 'Have you heard from. . .from Drew and the others?' she added quickly.

'Yes. Nothing to report,' was Tom's cheerful response. 'They've made camp not too far from you. A couple of miles.'

Made camp. A couple of miles. That meant she would definitely be alone tonight. And she still had to collect more wood upstream for the night's blaze as well as for heating her evening meal of tinned spaghetti and toast.

It *is* lonely here. Perhaps I shouldn't have been so confident this morning. Drew would laugh if he could see me now, she thought, her heart lurching uncomfortably as she remembered his kiss.

* * *

Drew *wasn't* laughing at that moment. Truth to tell, he was feeling distinctly irritable, and talked as little as he could while he ate his tinned beef stew. The day had been a long one. He and Alan had combed up and down several rocky gorges and gullies, using binoculars and calling out periodically. It was spectacular country, if he had had any time to enjoy it. Th myriad subtle variations in the hue of the rock, the two silently still waterholes they had found in deep, shaded gorges, the thin, splashing streams of Birradindi Falls that poured over a jagged lip of rock, fell fifty feet, then fanned into a pattern of lacy rivulets before feeding a clear, surprisingly cold pool.

He had doused his head under one of the streams to cool off, relishing the feel of the water thudding into his hair. A swim would have been nice. . .with Susan. . . He could almost see her poised on the edge of this pool in that alarmingly attractive dark red swimsuit she had appeared in a couple of months ago.

But of course there was no time even to be thinking about this. Towards dusk they had met up with Matt and Graham, creating several minutes of false hope as each pair had glimpsed the others in the distance and thought that they were two of the missing hikers.

'We came to a dead end,' Matt had reported, taking out a map that was by this time crumpled and dusty. 'The map doesn't show it, but this gorge is impassable at the far end, so we had to make a detour.'

'We may as well make camp together, then,' Drew had suggested, and now they had done so. In a way it was a good thing, as it gave him licence to remain within his own thoughts while the other three talked, but perhaps it would have been better if he had been forced to join in. . .

'How's Susan?' he asked Tom over the radio at seven.

'No worries, Drew. She seems pretty tough,' was Tom's casual response. Completely unsatisfying, and he didn't dare to ask for more details in case it gave away the fact that. . .

That fact that what? His train of thoughts came to a screeching halt as the answer hit him, and his heart was pounding. I'm in love with her! He had called his nagging awareness of her by a dozen other names—physical attraction, protectiveness, respect. . . And now, of all times, he had been hit with the truth like a physical blow. Now, when she was two and a half miles away, sitting alone by a fire and there was no way he could reach her tonight.

Or was there? With a torch he could probably cover the distance in an hour and a half or less.

You're tired, Drew! he told himself sternly. Susan is all right. What on earth would you do? Stagger into camp, throw yourself on her and tell her you love her? Yes, exactly that! His crazy determination grew, and when the stew was all gone he announced gruffly, 'I'm going back to camp.'

'Mate. . .?' began Matt in a questioning tone.

'Susan is alone,' he explained tersely. 'She's not the sort to complain, but she must be spooked. I'll join you again first thing in the morning.'

Matt was staring at him with narrowed eyes. 'Better OK it with Tom, hadn't you?'

'No need,' Drew replied firmly. He knew he was probably breaking one of the cardinal rules of search and rescue organisation, and he didn't care.

Matt nodded and held his tongue. Five minutes later, Drew was on his way.

Susan got the sleeping-bag and foam pad from her tent and brought them close to the fire. The blaze was her only companion tonight. She might as well doze beside it. It was still only ten.

But I should have got into this two hours ago, she thought.

For the first time, with the protective cocoon of

down and nylon around her, she wasn't pricking up her ears at every tiny sound, and suddenly she knew a feeling of quiet pride in how she had handled the day. It *hadn't* been easy. The feeling of solitude out here was so intense at times. But she had done everything she was delegated to do, and hadn't gone to pieces.

Now if only we could find those hikers. . .

She heard a sound, and this time it *wasn't* amplified by imagination. Something was there, and it was making the rhythmic sound of footsteps. She turned, saw a shape in the darkness and felt panic begin to rise in her throat. Then she recognised him. 'Drew!' She tried to move towards him, but the sleeping-bag had become a strait-jacket and she couldn't get out of it quickly enough. 'Have you found them? What's going on? Where's Alan?'

As he reached the fire, he dropped the pack he was carrying and sank to his knees in the red dirt. His legs were shaking, his hair was sweat-dampened and he was breathing very heavily. 'You're exhausted!' she accused.

'Yes.' He found breath to speak at last.

'Tell me, then! Do I need to call Tom?'

'You should. Not yet, though. To say I've arrived.'

'I still don't understand.' She searched his drained face.

And everything he had planned to say vanished from his mind. Away from her, it had seemed so simple. Now he doubted his own feelings—he had married once before on the strength of mere infatuation. This feeling was intense, but would it last? And hers, as well. In the white heat of his revelation he had assumed that she was burning with this too, but now. . .

In the sleeping-bag she looked so self-contained and so much more in control than even Tom's assessment of 'She seems pretty tough' allowed for. Realising all this, he then blurted the stupidest possible thing. 'I wanted to make sure you really were all right. Tom kept reporting that you were, but——'

'But you didn't believe it could be true,' she finished for him. Not for the first time, she interpreted his protectiveness as condescension and it angered her, made her feel less than his equal. 'It was an extremely dangerous thing to do, to walk through this terrain after dark. You could have been added to our list of people to search for.'

'I had to. I knew the route and I had a torch. We shouldn't have left you here alone. It's a very solitary place, Susan.'

'I'm good with solitude.'

'You're angry, aren't you?'

They looked at each other in the darkness, their faces lit only by the orange glow of fire. She saw tiredness and strain etched in his features and a question in his eyes which ran deeper than the one he had just asked her. She *had* been angry, but suddenly it left her and she said on a sigh, 'No, I'm not angry, Drew. Thank you for taking such a risk. It's good to have some company.'

His company, she meant. The soldier who had kissed her and left this morning had returned and she wished that she dared to snuggle close to him, but she didn't, and the sleeping-bag certainly didn't make it easier.

'Shall I put the kettle on?' she said.

'We have that drinking-chocolate powder, don't we?'

'Yes.'

'A cup of that would be great.'

The half-hour that followed was oddly important, although outwardly little happened. As they sipped the hot drinks they exchanged stories of the day, then Drew got out his sleeping-bag and slid inside it. 'That cold dew is falling,' he growled. 'Lie close to me. . .'

So she did, and the padded, down-filled shape of his sleeping-bag cocooned the padded, down-filled shape of hers so that even though they didn't touch she felt a

warmth and safety that sent her into a delicious sleep.
Perhaps. . .I do like being. . .protected after all, she
decided drowsily.

'Susan?' Drew was shaking her. Blinking in the daylight
and shifting her shoulders, she saw that he was already
dressed and that the hair at his temples was wet from
the refreshing splash he had given to his face.

'It's light,' he said. 'I have to get going.'

'Get going?'

'Yes, back to where the others are camped.'

Stupidly, she hadn't realised last night that he would
be returning there this morning, and the news came
like a dousing of icy water. 'Then. . .'

'I've already radioed to Tom. He says if there's no
sign of the hikers by noon you'll have to call for an
upscaled search.'

'OK. . .' She still wasn't awake enough to deal with
this.

'And I've had breakfast, so. . .'

'So you're off again right now?'

'Yes.'

'You should have woken me up before.'

'There was no need. I wanted to let you sleep. . .
Hey!' He had noticed the difficulty she was having.

'I'm all right. I just have to. . .' She began to struggle
out of the sleeping-bag. How could she explain to him
that last night had felt so safe she hadn't been thinking
beyond it at all, hadn't prepared herself for another
day of being alone.

He saw something of this in her face, though, and a
sound that was half-growl, half-groan came from deep
in his throat, dying away as he made her the willing
prisoner of his kiss. She responded hungrily and felt
hot tears pricking behind her eyes. This was hopeless.
This wasn't going to help. And she couldn't stop it. . .

His hair smelled of smoke and his neck of dust and
sweat. No doubt her own skin was the same. Beneath

her the ground no longer seemed hard, and she could have stayed this way for hours, touching the roughness of his unshaven jaw with her fingers, feeling the weight of him as he lay over her. But he pulled away and they both knew that this was not the right time to explore or to ask questions.

'If you can wait five minutes, I'll walk you a little way, shall I?' she said breathlessly. 'Just until you leave the line of the creek-bed.'

'I'd like that.' His voice was husky and dark-toned.

When she had splashed her face, drunk some water and put on shoes, they set off, walking in silence. Susan was afraid to break it. Something had happened. It was more than just awareness between them, although there was plenty of that. He was just ahead of her, his forearms tanned and strong where they emerged from rolled blue sleeves and his legs fit and muscular beneath sturdy jeans. He turned frequently to smile at her and she had to smile back as she felt heat and happiness well within her. It was almost as if he felt——

'Hello! Hello! Help! We're here! Oh, God, is someone there?'

Two voices, tumbling incoherently over each other, came at them out of the scrubby underbrush on the opposite bank of the creek and a moment later two people had appeared—a man and a woman—and Drew was immediately bounding across the dry river pebbles to reach them. Susan followed as fast as she could. It was two of the missing hikers, the man with a four-day growth of beard and the woman with her ankle bound up with a rough, dirty bandage.

'Thank God! Thank God!' they both said, almost sobbing.

'Your ankle. . .' Drew began.

'Sprained. Maybe broken. It's so painful. . . Happened the day before yesterday, but that's not important,' the woman answered. 'It's my father-in-law.'

'Do you have radio equipment? A team of searchers?

Medical help?' the man barked hoarsely. 'We think my father has had a heart attack.'

Hours of work, waiting and uncertainty followed. Bill Holland's suspected heart attack had happened three days ago at the furthest point of their route from the main camp, and as Mark and Debbie Holland gasped out their story they did not even know if he was still alive. Once Drew had radioed to Tom with the news, he set off alone to join the other searchers, his backpack loaded with medical gear and a portable stretcher.

'Call the Flying Doctor,' he told Susan, 'but tell them there's no point in getting here for at least five hours. . .'

Meanwhile, she treated Debbie Holland's ankle, and treated both Debbie and Mark for exhaustion and some dehydration, doing all she could to get them to rest in spite of their anxiety. Finally, the word came from Tom by radio—Bill Holland and his son Jonathan had been found, both alive and in good spirits.

'The Flying Doctor plane will be here by one o'clock, Tom,' Susan was able to report in return.

'Hope you did a good job of clearing that strip. . .'

'So do I!'

The two Holland men were both exhausted when they reached camp, as were the six men who had searched and hiked so tirelessly for a day and a half. Bill Holland had needed the stretcher, and would be flown all the way to Perth by the Flying Doctor plane, as his symptoms did point to a potentially serious heart condition. Debbie would accompany him on the flight, as her ankle injury was quite severe, compounded as it had been by two days of heavy walking.

Once the plane had taken off with the two patients, all that remained to be done was to clear and pack up the camp before setting off for Coolacoola. Tom and Matt would drive together, while the other searchers would take turns at the wheel of the hikers' Toyota, as

Mark and Jonathan were both too exhausted to drive. Susan and Drew climbed into the medical centre's four-wheel drive.

'It'll be dark by the time we get home,' the latter commented as they began the trip.

'Dark? I suppose it will. I've lost track of time,' Susan confessed.

'My stomach hasn't. We barely remembered to eat today.'

'There are still some sandwiches. Stale, but——'

'I don't care!'

Somehow the journey seemed much shorter today than it had two nights ago. It *was* a little shorter in the daylight, but this didn't fully account for Susan's feelings. It's because I'm alone with Drew, she realised, and I don't want it to end.

Not that he kissed her again, nor even that they talked. Both were too tired. But just to have him beside her. . . When he drove, she was aware of the dynamism that overlaid his fatigue, the way his shoulders worked the steering-wheel and the way his narrowed eyes took in every obstacle and change of direction ahead of the scratchy track. When he ceded the wheel to her, she just had enough attention left over from her own concentration on the route to be aware of his long body slumped diagonally across the seat as he allowed his weariness to overtake him at last. And after several more minutes, when she risked a glance at his face, she saw that he slept. . .

Jane Arnold and Margaret Latham were both waiting for the returning searchers back at Coolacoola. They had kept in touch by radio over the past two days, and Simon and Jeremy had both followed the unfolding drama with a child's zest for adventure.

'You poor love!' Jane said to Susan, taking her arm and coaxing her inside the head ranger's comfortable house. 'There are casseroles in the oven, but you need a shower first?'

'Do I smell that bad?'

Everyone laughed and Jane came in quickly, 'No, no, but——'

Drew cut her off with a gruff, 'Look at your clothes, Susan.'

His were the same—streaked with red dust, marked black in parts by smoke and charcoal, limp, crumpled and dust-filled. Tom and Matt too looked stained and drooping.

'I think I'm too hungry to wait for a shower,' Susan confessed.

'But, Drew, I bet *you're* not too hungry to wait for this,' Jane came in. 'News from Melbourne. Your sister-in-law had healthy triplet girls this morning, and they expect to come up here for a holiday, as planned, in about two months! Triplets! I can't wait!'

CHAPTER NINE

THOSE two months had almost passed, when Susan herself had a visitor. 'Dad!' She stood up from behind her desk in the reception area of the medical centre, her legs suddenly weak with surprise.

It *was* her father! At first she hadn't even been sure. Six years had changed him a lot, and the diffidence of his approach had cast a doubt as well.

It was noon and the medical centre's fortnightly baby clinic was about to end. Drew was on call to deal with any more serious medical questions that emerged, but he hadn't been needed this morning and it had been a very happy, very female time.

Babies had been measured and weighed, earnest discussions had taken place on such surprisingly complex topics as nappy rash, weaning, teething and cradle cap. The women always used the clinic as a gossip session and friendly get-together, and a strange male's sudden intrusion into all this had created confusion all round.

Ankala and Andara Zebulon, whose fat, healthy babies were both nearly four months old now, departed among a squealing cluster of children, and an aboriginal woman from a cattle station about forty kilometres away made a quieter departure with her two-month-old boy.

'What are you doing here?' Susan was able to say at last. Then, because it hadn't sounded very friendly, 'I mean, why didn't you let me know?'

He came up to her and they hugged awkwardly, each relieved when the gesture was done with. 'I could have, I suppose,' he said. 'Wanted to surprise you. Got sent up here at short notice, you see, and——'

'Sent?'

'Yes. The company. They've had some cost overruns at Jambarra recently, and——'

'Jambarra Mine?'

'Yes. . . Oh, I dare say you didn't know. Minex
International is one of our subsidiaries.' He explained
a little further and Susan nodded, only taking half of it
in.

She was thinking, A convenient way to combine
business with duty. He must have looked at a map,
seen how close it was, borrowed a mine vehicle. . .

A covert glance out of the window told her that this
last part was correct. A dust-coated white vehicle with
Minex International's black and red lettering was
parked crookedly out at the front. But their relationship was too distant for her even to feel pain or anger
at his offhandedness any more, and over the past six
years their lack of communication had been as much
her own fault as his.

She didn't make an issue of it, therefore, saying
simply instead, 'You can stay to lunch, can't you? I'm
finished here now. We can go across to my house and
make sandwiches. Soup, too, if you like.'

'Sandwiches sound fine,' he said. 'I can stay for
about an hour, then I have to get back. I have a
meeting with the mine management at two. These cost
overruns. . .'

'Mm, it must be difficult.'

She locked up the building and they crossed the short
distance to her house along the covered walkway. He
seemed to approve of the place, she noted as she made
sandwiches of ham and lettuce and mustard. He was
pacing about, examining various objects, and finally,
just as the simple meal was ready, he turned to her and
said, 'Are you happy here, Sue?'

She hated, 'Sue' and always had, but let it slip by.
He had meant it as an endearment. 'Yes, I am.'

'It was a big change. I was surprised when I got your

letter. Thought you were ensconced in that house of
Dot's for life.'

'It suits me here. At the moment. I won't stay here
forever. But I may not go back to Melbourne, either.'
Wider horizons had been beckoning of late, both
physical and emotional ones.

'I wondered if—er—love troubles had sent you
away.'

'No, nothing like that.' Here at Coolacoola, of
course, there was the ongoing heartache of Drew. Was
he a 'love trouble'? Not one to talk about now, anyway.

'It made me feel as if I ought to have tried harder six
years ago to get you to come to Perth,' her father went
on. He had obeyed her gesture to sit at the table and
had taken a sandwich, but it now sat in his hand,
untouched and halfway to his mouth.

Susan sat down as well. 'No, Dad. . .' she said
slowly. 'It wouldn't have worked.'

'You don't think so?'

'You had Kirsty and the girls.'

'But you're my daughter too. . .although I've been a
bad father to you, I know.'

Should she agree with him? 'You did the best you
could at the time,' she managed. 'Perhaps some people
might have been able to do more. . .' Again she was
thinking of Drew and the struggle he had had over
Simon. 'But you knew that you couldn't, so——'

'So I left you with your aunt. She begged to have
you, in fact.'

'She did?' This was something that Susan hadn't
known.

'Yes, and it seemed so easy. I meant to take you
back eventually, but time went on, and I met Kirsty. . .
I just let things slide. You seemed happy enough with
Dot.'

Had she been happy? Susan wondered. Not miserable, certainly. Aunty Dot had never been wilfully
cruel. But her eccentricity at times had bordered on

harshness and had certainly imprisoned Susan in a lifestyle that gave her little in common with other girls of her age. Her aunt's obsessive punctuality, her suspicion of strangers, the wholesale rejection of fashion and television and other 'evils' of the modern world, those ticking clocks each set five minutes fast. . .

Susan now realised that her father had probably never glimpsed most of this eccentricity. Was there any point in telling him? No. . .'I was happy for most of the time,' she told him. 'And I'm happy with who I am now, so isn't that all that matters?'

'Yes. . .' He took a bite of his sandwich at last and gave an unconscious sigh, as if acknowledging to himself that she had let him off the hook.

For the rest of the meal they talked about Coolacoola, and about Kirsty and the girls, and he finished by saying, 'You must get some leave and a ticket to Perth at some point, surely?'

'Yes, after six months, but I think I'll wait until the really hot weather before I use it.'

'Come down to us. I think you'd like the girls. You should get to know them. They are your half-sisters, after all.'

'I will come,' she answered him, and meant it. No doubt such a visit would have its tensions, but she felt able to face them now. Coolacoola has changed me, she realised, although she did not voice the thought aloud.

Ten minutes later, Bruce Carstairs was ready to leave. He had brought a briefcase with him, and now he opened it to bring out a soft, light package wrapped in gold paper. 'I know it was your birthday a few days ago,' he said. 'I knew I was coming up so I didn't send the usual card. Here. . . Happy twenty-fourth. Kirsty picked it out.'

Susan tore open the shimmering wrapping and found a dress—simple and slippery and silky and black. A cocktail dress. Gorgeous, actually, but where on earth would she wear it out here? 'Thanks, Dad.'

'Kirsty picked it out,' he said again as she kissed him on the cheek, and then their arms were around each other and he was squeezing her tightly. 'You look so good. . . You've done well. I'm proud of you, Sue.'

As she watched him drive away a few minutes later, Susan found that her eyes were blurred by tears. Wouldn't it be strange if coming to Coolacoola actually gave her a father again after all these years?

It had given Simon Kershaw a father, apparently. While she still stood there on the veranda, Susan saw Drew and Simon going past towards the Lathams' house. They waved at her then passed on. The little boy usually had lunch at home with Drew, unless the latter was too busy with work. Drew would collect him from the Arnold house and take him to Margaret Latham, and in between they always had a marvellous hour, to judge from the child's happy face as he walked along holding his father's hand.

No, *not* his father. Not biologically. Did Drew think of this fact often? She didn't know. They seemed to avoid any subject that was too close to the bone these days when they talked. Had done, in fact, since those two days out at Birradindi Creek, which were now nearly two months ago. Not what she had expected. Back then, the drama, the isolation and the kisses that had exploded between them seemed to be bringing them closer, but now he was keeping her at arm's length and she could only accept it.

In fact, she told herself that she was glad of it. The closeness of friendship could be very painful when you wanted love, she had found. Sometimes she wondered whether the situation would become intolerable one day, forcing her to leave Coolacoola. She didn't want to leave the place for such a reason. In fact, at the moment she didn't want to leave the place at all.

Would you like it so much if Drew weren't here? a

sly inner voice asked. Watching him disappear down the street, the lines of his figure so taut and masculine from the rear, Susan didn't dare to examine the issue too closely. . .

'It's been the most wonderful break, Drew,' Kate Kershaw told her brother-in-law late one warm night in early October.

They were sitting on the veranda together. Drew had bought some foldable wood and canvas outdoor chairs on a recent visit to Pendleton, and it was very comfortable out here now. His brother Charles had gone to bed already, as had Kate's mother, who had come up to Coolacoola to help with the three babies during the ten-day holiday.

It was after midnight, and Kate had just settled the tiny girls down after an evening feed. Drew had only recently gone off duty as well. A child staying out at the camping ground had had a severe fever and other symptoms, and he had been called out to examine the three-year-old. Now it would be sensible if both of them went to bed, but somehow the sense of peacefulness and the chance of quiet conversation was too good to pass up.

'I'm glad you've enjoyed it,' Drew responded to Kate's comment. 'I was afraid you might find it too tiring.'

'Less tiring than at home, with Mum here and Charles on hand instead of at work. You've all pampered me, and those walks and swims we've had! After the months in bed, I've got a body I can use again at last!'

'The bed-rest was worth every minute, wasn't it?'

'Drew, do you need to ask?'

They both laughed, then sat in silence for a minute. Kate had something on her mind. Drew was sure of it—an intuition born of the fact that he had something on his mind as well, only he had no idea how he could possibly talk about it, nor even if he wanted to.

'It's tough, though,' Kate went on at last. 'Three babies, and our garden and the hens and goats to look after.'

'Not to mention the other assorted creatures in your menagerie.'

'Mum can't keep on giving us so much time, so we've decided to get a full-time nanny-housekeeper if we can.'

'That'll be good,' Drew answered a little absently. He couldn't quite work out what she was leading up to here, and was distracted by wondering, for no reason at all, whether Susan was soundly asleep at this moment.

'Which means——' Kate took a deep breath, leaned forward and fixed Drew in the eye, recapturing his attention instantly '—we can take Simon again if you'd like us to.'

'Take Simon?' He could only echo the words blankly. It had never occurred to him that Kate and Charles were thinking of this.

'I miss him an enormous amount, you see. We both do,' Kate explained apologetically. 'And now that things are settling into a routine with the triplets. . . You've been lucky here so far that arrangements have worked out well for Simon's care, but——'

'No!' he said, and the word had a strangled quality to it. 'No, Kate! It's out of the question.'

He hadn't even realised that he felt this strongly about it. The reaction was purely an emotional one, taking him completely by surprise with its force and certainty. It was months now since he had felt even a glimmering of the anger that he had been so afraid of, and this gave him a satisfaction whenever he thought about it—which he didn't often. Simon, these days, was simply Simon, beloved for himself and without regard for any abstract biological link, or lack of one.

'You sound very sure,' Kate was saying. 'I'm glad.
Don't be angry at my suggestion, Drew. I just want
what's best for him.'

'Yes. . .' Drew *hadn't* been thinking that unselfishly
himself. Was Coolacoola best for the little boy? 'What's
best for Simon. Of course that's the most important
thing. I'll ask him what he wants, and we won't make
a final decision until then.'

'Drew, I didn't mean——'

'No, no, you're right. I've been assuming he would
be happiest here with me, but after all. . .'

'Damn, I've upset you now, haven't I?' his sister-in-
law muttered.

'No, not upset. You've given me food for thought.
After all, I'm just one man. You and Charles and the
triplets are a family. Perhaps he should have that. . .'

'Look, I shouldn't have said anything!' She got up
and paced to the edge of the veranda, then said with
her back to him, 'As for the family thing. . .is it so
impossible to think that you might form a family again
soon?'

'Me? Form a family?' It was a startled, almost
bleating echo.

'Yes. Susan. She seems delightful. . . I'm being blunt
again. . . Very different from Lisa, but perhaps this
time that's what you need.'

'Kate. . .' Susan was the subject he had wanted to
discuss with her, but now that she had brought it up he
shrank from it.

'Sorry. I can't help it, Drew. We're leaving tomorrow
and we both care so much about you. If Simon is going
to stay here with you—and I think, really, that he
should—then I have to know if you're happy, and what
you're planning.'

'I'm not planning anything,' he growled.

'But you're in love with her.'

He didn't answer. Why had Charles married such a
busybody? And she wouldn't leave the subject alone.

'You *are*, Drew!' She had turned to him again and the words were almost an accusation. The recent birth had given her body a new fullness and strength and her slight figure was quite imposing as her gaze bore down upon him.

'What's motherhood done to you, Kate?' he responded helplessly. 'Turned you into an amateur personal guidance counsellor?'

'In this case, yes,' she insisted. 'Since it concerns two people I love—you and Simon. Now, I want the truth!'

'I'd tell you if I knew,' he said.

'You *do* know, but you're holding back. Why?'

There was quite a pause, then, 'I'm afraid,' he admitted. 'To make that commitment again. Afraid of. . .of an error in judgement.'

'Hmm. . .'

There was another silence and he dreaded that she would fill it with questions about Lisa. One day, perhaps, he would tell Kate and Charles the truth about the unhappiness of his marriage, but not now. He and Lisa had both hidden it from them rather well. . .

'How long has this been going on?' Kate asked.

'You mean how long have I. . .?'

'How long have you loved her?' Painfully blunt once again.

'Oh, since. . .' He laughed. 'Do you want the exact date?'

'Of course not!'

He didn't tell her that if she did he could provide it—that evening at Birradindi Creek when he hadn't been able to stand the idea of her spending the night alone. He said instead, 'Since just around the time that the triplets were born.'

'Two months. And you haven't said anything to her?'

'No, I. . . As I said, I——'

'Then perhaps you're right. It can't be important

enough. If you're willing to run the risk of losing her—'

'*Losing* her?'

'Yes! She's not going to wait forever, you know! I suspect that you're the first person to awaken her to love, but that doesn't mean you'll be the last. Some hunky young mining company geologist, or. . . Didn't Tom Arnold say they're taking on another park ranger, a single man? Probably just her type—outdoorsy and a little bit shy but very masculine in the best possible way.'

'Kate!' he growled. Perversely, he was irked by her sketched notion of what would be Susan's 'type', since the description didn't fully fit himself. 'Stop!'

And, much to his surprise, she did, spreading her hands as if to say, I've said my piece. Make of it what you will. Seeing the wide, uncontrollable yawn that she hid behind her hand seconds later, he told her, 'Go to bed! Those babies will want feeding again in another two hours or so.'

'I know.' She smiled, yawned again, apologised, wished him a goodnight, and disappeared inside.

Drew himself was even less ready for bed than he had been half an hour ago. Kate had gone, but she had left someone behind—a shadowy figure who could have been a geologist, or could have been a park ranger—and Drew felt an absurd urge to shove the man off this veranda and say to him, You're trespassing!

It hadn't occurred to him that Susan might some day soon be attracted to someone else. Arrogant, that! He had assumed that his own doubts were the only obstacles to conquer. And now Kate's words chafed at him. She'd said that he'd probably awakened her to love. . . but that he might lose her. Nonsense, wasn't it? He had no proof in the first place that he *had* awakened anything in her, he realised. Added to his lack of confidence in what he felt himself. . . Wouldn't it be better if the whole thing just faded away?

Something inside him answered this question with a rebellious, resounding. No! and he was shaking as he got up and half staggered down the veranda steps, not stopping until he reached the point where he could see her darkened house beyond the medical centre. This feeling fade away? No!

'I'm such an idiot!' he hissed aloud between clenched teeth. 'Kate's right! I might lose her. Is that something I want to risk?'

'There'll be tennis and swimming in the afternoon,' said Elaine Hamilton as she prepared to leave Coolacoola's medical centre after a routine prenatal visit. Her due date was just a month away now, 'Then a barbecue. Then we'll all get dressed up and have a dance, so bring something really nice. City fashion, please! I hunger for it sometimes.'

'Next Saturday, you said? It sounds wonderful,' Susan answered.

'Short notice, I know. But we decided on an impulse and wanted to have it before the new baby, and before the really hot weather. Drew and Simon are coming, of course, and the Arnolds and the Lathams. . .' She listed numerous other people, some of whom would be flying hundreds of miles from other cattle stations in their own light planes.

'Can I bring anything?'

'Just yourself. . .'

'And all the right clothes for tennis and swimming and dancing. I'll have to pack a suitcase!' Susan laughed.

She was pleased at the invitation. Since the departure of the triplets and their entourage two days ago, things at Coolacoola had seemed a little flat. Drew had been withdrawn and thoughtful, and she assumed he was missing his brother's family, so had trodden very carefully around him, respecting what she interpreted as a desire to be left alone. But perhaps he would look forward to this big pärty too, and it would cheer him up. Everyone said Namburra Downs was so beautiful. . .but of course Drew had been there before, three times, to visit Patsy Strickland.

I expect that really *will* cheer him up, Susan decided sensibly. The chance to see her again. . .

Everyone was looking forward to the event, it seemed. Margaret came round that night to ask, 'Do you have a tennis dress?' and, when Susan's answer was an apologetic no the deputy ranger's wife produced white cotton fabric and three packets of sewing patterns and began to delve into the question of style on the spot.

'In five days?' Susan protested. 'It'll never be ready in time.'

'Yes, it will! And now for the evening dance. . .'

But here Susan was already prepared—the black dress chosen by her young stepmother Kirsty. Not for the first time, she felt a moment of tentative warmth and hope as she thought about the visit to Perth that her father had suggested. Margaret's reaction to Susan's modelling of the garment was gratifying. 'My goodness, I hope Elaine Hamilton has got some good single men coming! We can't let *this* go to waste!'

'Can't we?' Susan laughed. The dress, swirling around her as she pirouetted for Margaret, did feel wonderful.

'No, indeed! Now, let's see. . . If the contingent from Walker's Creek comes. . . They've got a manager there now and he's single. About thirty, I think. . .'

Susan let her talk on, aware that Margaret and Jane had a friendly little conspiracy to get her involved with a man, and married if at all possible. So far two candidates had been presented—a friend of Jane's from Perth who had come to Coolacoola for a week's hiking, and the new junior park ranger, who had come for an interview with Tom and would be returning to start work at the park in a month's time.

Both men had been very nice, and Susan had tried her best to fall madly in love with each of them on the spot, but it hadn't worked. *I'll have to get Drew Kershaw out of my system first,* she had realised, and she was beginning to suspect that the only way to do this was to leave. It created a great big question mark over the future that she didn't like one bit. It would be much easier to fall in with Margaret and Jane's happy plans.

'You'll drive to Namburra Downs with us on Saturday, won't you, Susan?' Drew said to her the next day, very casually, during their twice-weekly morning session of administrative work.

'Yes, that seems sensible, doesn't it?' she agreed calmly. 'No sense in bringing both vehicles.'

'No, none at all.'

A typically bland, friendly exchange, and they went on to agree that he would pick her up straight after lunch.

The following Saturday, he arrived promptly at one-thirty. . .and Susan wasn't ready. She had pottered around happily that morning, packing clothes and swimming things into an overnight bag and ironing the tropical print blouse that she would team with plain blue jeans for the drive and the barbecue. The new tennis dress had needed to be collected from Margaret's, and the latter hadn't hemmed it yet, so pinning it and sewing the hem by hand had taken a little time.

Washing her hair, blow-waving some bounce into the short, pretty bob, choosing accessories for the evening, making a sandwich for lunch. . . She was humming over the washing-up when Drew's knock sounded, convinced that it was only just after one, and her feet were still bare of the tan sandals she wanted to wear.

Padding to the door, it occurred to her that this had

never happened before. In fact, she could almost see another Susan sitting stiffly beside the kitchen table, a frowning glance glued to her watch and the overnight bag already clutched tightly in her hands. That other Susan was very envious of this new one at first, to judge by her tense stare, then she carefully took one hand off the overnight bag, smiled at the new Susan, and gave a thumbs-up sign.

'Why are you laughing?' Drew asked as she opened the door to him.

'Oh, just a private joke between me and the person I used to be,' she told him saucily, and refused to explain any further. It would have sounded ridiculous. Precisely two and three-quarter minutes later, she was ready to leave, and the world—which Aunty Dot had always led her to believe might come to an end in such a circumstance—still appeared to be spinning on schedule.

Spinning. . . Susan felt very giddy that afternoon. It seemed that everyone within a radius of hundreds of miles had come to Namburra Downs for the party. Children of all ages splashed in the pool or played hide-and-seek through the rambling desert garden. Adults sat in the shade watching the tennis, or took their turn on the court, and there was a changing roster of volunteers as well, helping in the kitchen, finishing the decorations for the dance, and looking after the children.

Susan took part in everything, and was very glad of the space that had been set aside as a ladies' changing-room as she slipped into her tennis dress, wriggled into her swimsuit and then pulled on jeans and blouse again to explore by herself for a little while before volunteering her help to Mrs Hamilton.

Drew found her by the aviary at the far end of the garden. 'What's wrong?'

'Nothing,' she answered cheerfully. 'I'm exploring, that's all. It really is gorgeous, isn't it? The oleander and the bottle-brush and kangaroo-paw. The birds. I've counted eight kinds of parrot and cockatoo flying about in this aviary, and it's huge! And with the pepper-trees and couch-grass everywhere it seems so cool. . .'

'Yes it's been well-designed so it doesn't use too much water. These hedges and latticed fences keep away some of the direct sun and most of the drying winds. We must get some shrubs started around the medical centre. We should ask Elaine for suggestions.'

'Yes, she obviously knows a lot about what will grow best out here.'

'Have you seen it all yet?'

'No. I haven't looked at the farm buildings, or the garden beyond the tennis court at all, except what I could glimpse as I was playing.'

'Do you want some more tennis? That's what I was looking for you to ask you, actually. They want a final set before drinks and the barbecue. Patsy Strickland is going to partner Sam Bellamy from Walker's Creek and I volunteered you and me as their opponents. You'd just have time to change again before the present set finishes.'

He was leaning casually against the wire mesh of the aviary in his white tennis shorts and shirt, and suddenly the sounds from the court and the pool seemed very distant. Even the chatter and rustle of the birds in the aviary was only a background murmur. Her awareness of him, which she mostly succeeded in pushing aside, surged in this lovely private spot and she had to answer very quickly before she betrayed herself in trembling lips and an uncontrollable sway towards him.

'I'd love another set,' she said. 'I'll go and change right now.'

She hurried ahead of him and disappeared into the ladies' changing-room without another word. When she emerged again, with the flared skirt below the drop-waist of the new tennis dress still fresh-looking as

it swung against her lightly tanned thighs, Drew had
gone and she guessed that he would be at the court
already, joining the other onlookers.

The court was more shaded now than it had been
earlier, when she had narrowly lost a doubles set with
Matt Latham against two strangers from a cattle station
a hundred miles away. In the open brushwood pavilion
that overlooked the rectangle of artificial grass, a
cluster of onlookers already had long cool drinks and
most had changed from tennis to barbecue gear now.

As Susan caught sight of Drew among the group,
there was a shout of appreciation and a burst of
applause and the current set ended in a spectacular
winning stroke. Brian Hamilton left the court swearing.
'This damned hand!' And as he passed Drew he said,
'Doc, talk to me again about that plastic surgeon. I
can't get used to this!'

'Whenever you like, Brian,' Drew answered, and his
eyes met Susan's in shared satisfaction.

Seconds later, Patsy Strickland unwound her long
legs from an outdoor chair, called to her partner Sam
Bellamy from Walker's Creek and ambled lazily on to
the court. Drew tossed a racket to Susan and they
joined the other pair to warm up and play for serve.

'You and I won our set, Drew,' Patsy called across
the black and white net. 'But we can't both win this
time!'

The governess from Namburra Downs was a good
player, Susan soon found. She herself had been pleased
with her performance earlier. At school she had been
quite a tidy, useful doubles partner, but she hadn't
played since and had expected to be rustier. But
perhaps that first set had just been beginner's luck,
because now she couldn't seem to do a thing. Patsy
flashed around the court in her brief, tight shorts and
sleeveless blouse, and her partner cracked out serve
after punishing serve like gunfire.

Drew's encouraging calls of, 'Go for it, Susan,' and,

'I'll get this,' became heartier and heartier until, when the game score was four-love to the other pair, she finally said to him in an intense, low murmur, 'I know I'm playing like an elephant. Don't keep encouraging me. It's only making me worse!'

'Sorry,' he growled. His face, like hers, was hot, lightly freckled, and beaded with sweat. She wanted to find a piece of dry towelling and wipe it from him. 'I'm trying to let you know that it doesn't matter. Your face and stance look as if you're losing a Wimbledon final.'

'They do?'

'Yes, and it was Patsy who threw out that challenge about only one of us winning, not me. Do you think I care? You looked so fresh before in that seductive little dress. I wanted to be your partner because——' He stopped abruptly and swished his racket through the air to make a hard, resonant hum. 'Well, I was looking forward to being your partner. That's all. Now, let's relax.'

'I'll try.' She went to the net and turned to watch him serve against the background of wire mesh and soft green acacia foliage beyond.

He stretched high, hit the ball sweetly in the centre of the racket then ran forward on light feet to follow through on the return from Patsy with a force that looked effortless. Seconds later, it was Susan's turn to tuck a clever net shot tightly into the nearest corner of the opposite court, and they had won the point. At the end of her own serve, suddenly and miraculously much more fluid now, they had brought the game score to four-three.

'Change ends,' called a man from the brushwood pavilion, who was acting as unofficial umpire.

Then, cutting across his voice, came running footsteps and cries of 'Help, help!' in a ten-year-old's urgent voice.

'What is it, love?' called out one of the women.

'A kid's been hurt. They were all playing with some

of the tools. He's only little, and he's bleeding a lot.
It's spurting. It's scary. Someone better come.'

'Drew?' someone called from the pavilion.

'Yes, of course.'

He dropped his racket and so did Susan, and she
caught Patsy's murmur of, 'Damn! There goes our set!'
She saw how white the boy looked and judged the
situation from that more than from what he had said.
Kids brought up in the outback on a cattle station
didn't look that colour—almost green—at the sight of
a cut finger or a stubbed toe.

'Where?' Drew was saying, against a background of
curious and anxious voices:

'Not my Jamie?'

'I'll come too. They may need more help.'

'Don't let's get in the way. Dr Kershaw knows what
he's going.'

'Up behind the big shed,' the red-headed ten-year-
old was saying. 'A big kid got the door open of where
they put all the tools. Some kids were boasting about
what they could do, how they helped their dads with
saws and axes and stuff. There were two big kids—the
ones Mrs Hamilton put in charge—telling them to be
careful and not to play with the stuff, but this little kid
slipped with the axe and. . .'

A few moments later, they saw the cluster of alarmed
children. An older girl was giving orders which were
being ignored as the group made erratic progress
towards the house. Two more older children were
carrying an ominously limp bundle of limbs. Several
voices were raised in frightened howls and blood was
everywhere.

Then Drew caught sight of the child's red-stained
pair of denim shorts and yellow T-shirt, and rasped out
just as Susan herself realised it, 'My God! That's
Simon!'

CHAPTER TEN

THE bright, spurting flow of arterial blood was strong and unceasing, literally draining the child's life away as they watched. Susan did not need Drew's barked orders to her. Before he had begun to speak she had started to sprint to the medical centre's four-wheel drive to open the medical chest in the back that contained sterile dressings among its many supplies.

Inside the house now, Drew took the thick gauze pad from her and pressed it to the thigh of his child with the firm weight of the heel of his hand. Simon was lying on a couch, his legs elevated thirty degrees and his body covered in a blanket. His skin was cool and clammy, his breathing came in rapid, shallow pants, and when Susan reached to take his pulse she found it weak and thready.

'Don't waste time on his pulse. We know he's in shock. Call the Flying Doctor,' Drew rasped. His face was grey. 'Use the radio in the car. They may already have a plane in our sector that they can divert. He needs to get to hospital. If I can't control this bleeding with pressure and we have to tourniquet, he could lose the leg. I could try to suture it on the spot, but it's a mess in there. . .'

Susan was profoundly thankful for her familiarity with the radio equipment. It took only a few minutes to make the call to the Royal Flying Doctor Service headquarters, find out that there was a plane in the area and contact it to supply details.

'Will he need transfusion?' the doctor—not Max Greeley, but a newer man—wanted to know.

'I think so, yes. He's lost a lot of blood.'

'Can you find out his blood group? Then we can make sure it's available.'

Drew would know. It was the first question she flung to him after she had told him that the plane was on its way. But Drew did *not* know and, for the first time, panic seemed to break through his outer competence and control.

'I must know. . . I should. Oh, God, why don't I?' he said hoarsely, holding a shaking hand to his pale forehead. 'It's never come up. It must be recorded somewhere. . .on the forms from the hospital when he was born, but. . . I can't remember——!'

'Would Charles and Kate know?' Susan interrupted urgently.

'Yes. Kate is very thorough. He had his tonsils out last year——'

'I'll phone them at once.'

'If they're not home——'

'I'll worry about that if it happens,' she told him firmly, touching the hard shape of his shoulder.

Kate *was* home, and Susan woke her from an afternoon rest, but that scarcely mattered once the other woman had heard the news. 'Is he going to be all right?' she demanded.

'Yes.' It was emphasised with more confidence than Susan really felt at this moment. 'Drew thinks the injury itself will be easy to repair in an operating theatre under general anaesthesia. No serious muscle or nerve damage. It's just the pain and the bleeding, and I need to know his blood group, so——'

'Transfusion?'

'Almost certainly.'

'It's the same as Drew's, Group A, but. . . Hang on. . .' She returned after only a few moments. 'Yes, I was right. When he had his tonsils out they told us that he has the Duffy antigen as well.'

'The Duffy antigen? That's pretty uncommon.'

'So they told us.'

'Thanks, Kate. That information will help with cross-matching. No time to talk now. I've got to find out if there's a supply of that group available in Pendleton.'

'Look after him, Susan,' Kate told her urgently. 'Look after both of them!'

'I will.' She rang off and phoned the hospital in Pendleton at once.

'Group A, with the Duffy antigen?' was the response. 'We'll have to fly it up from Perth, and even so. . .'

'There may be another option,' Susan told the woman on the other end of the line. 'The child's father's blood is the same, apparently.'

'We'll each follow through, then, and see what we come up with.'

'And we should be arriving with you in about an hour.'

'Standing by. . .'

The plane could already be heard overhead as Susan returned to Drew. 'I think I've stopped it,' he said. 'Muscle spasm in the artery walls had closed it.'

'The plane. . .'

'I know.'

Simon had already been placed on a stretcher, and now Drew and Brian Hamilton carried him out to the medical centre's vehicle for the half-mile drive out to the well-groomed airstrip. Susan took the wheel with damp, cold hands.

The little boy was disorientated, in pain, weakened and confused, and Drew did not leave his side for a second during the short journey, holding his hand and murmuring repetitive, reassuring words. For the moment the issue of transfusion was forgotten. The throng of people at Namburra Downs was just a background blurr, and the good wishes of those who had been helping just a meaningless babble.

The engine of the Flying Doctor aircraft was still roaring as Simon was carried aboard, Drew following immediately and then Susan, taking the two overnight bags that Elaine Hamilton thrust into her arms at the last moment, without even stopping to wonder what they were for. On the plane, Dr David Little and Sister Christine Bartlett worked quickly, replacing the dressing, setting up a drip and getting a stronger stream of normal saline and albumen flowing into the little boy's veins. . .

'Will there be blood waiting for him in Pendleton? He'll need it,' Dr Little said to Drew after observing the dangerously low blood-pressure and thready pulse. The plane's engine had screamed as it revved up and now they were airborne. Neither Susan nor anyone else had been aware of it happening.

'Susan?' Drew rasped.

'His group is A, and he has the Duffy antigen. It will need to be flown up from Perth and they're not sure that there's any available there either. But Kate said——'

'The Duffy antigen?' Drew cut urgently across her words. 'Kate said he had the Duffy antigen?'

'Yes. She looked it up. When he had his tonsils out——'

'That's impossible!'

'She thought that you had it too.'

'I do,' he answered her in a strangled tone, and for the first time she caught the implication that Drew had seized on at once. Simon and Drew shared a blood group and a rare blood antigen. . .yet Drew was not the child's biological father, or so he had believed for three and a half years.

'Then we can use you as a donor,' Dr Little was saying, oblivious to the undercurrents of realisation. 'We can set that up here and now.'

'Yes, of course.' Drew's response was so dazed that Susan was afraid for a moment that he was about to faint.

His arm was limp as Sister Bartlett swabbed the

inner crook of his forearm with antiseptic and cuffed
the upper arm tightly to bring a vein to prominence.
Moments later he was lying back as red fluid drained
from his arm into a bag with a strong, steady flow.

'Susan,' he whispered. 'Lisa was lying. It never
occurred to me. She was *lying* about Craig being——'
He stopped abruptly. This was not a subject to speak
of aloud in front of near-strangers. But in the background the plane vibrated with noise from the engines,
and the other doctor and nurse were still busy. They
weren't listening.

Susan hadn't needed him to complete the phrase.
'But *why*?'

'Who knows? I can only guess. Just to hurt me?
No. . . It was something more cold-blooded than that,'
he went on slowly. 'She wanted to stop me from
seeking custody. Perhaps she even hoped I wouldn't
ask for access. And she thought that if I believed he
wasn't mine, then I *wouldn't* ask for access. . . It might
even have worked, too. . .'

He didn't say any more, and neither did Susan. The
weight of this revelation was too enormous. It had
taken Drew over three years to lose his fear of loving
Simon and his fear of harming the child, but here in
the outback he *had* conquered the demon and now it
seemed that the demon was just a paper tiger. Simon
had been fully his all along, and Lisa's lie had cost him
the best solace he could have had for the messy and
tragic end to his failed marriage. If he lost Simon
altogether through today's accident. . .

'How are his blood-pressure and pulse now?' Susan
asked her fellow nurse urgently.

'Improving. Ninety over forty, and one hundred.
We'll need that blood. And plasma, too. The surgery
is going to strain his system.'

'How much longer will we be in the air?'

'Half an hour, then it's only a five-minute drive to
the hospital.'

'Thank God!'

'But is *he* going to be all right?' The nurse lowered her voice and gestured discreetly at Drew, who lay back with a hand over his eyes, his sensitive lips visible only as a tight, tension-filled line.

'I don't know. . .'

The flight seemed endless, but was over at last and an ambulance screamed through the pretty coastal town to the small but modern hospital. At the casualty department's ambulance bay, a small group of people was waiting to whisk Simon into surgery, and to take Drew's blood for cross-matching so that it could be ready as soon as possible.

'Don't forget these,' Christine Bartlett said to Susan, pushing the two overnight bags into her hands.

But Susan was too busy watching Drew! *Was* he going to faint? Once again it looked as if he might. His face was so white that the warm brown scattering of freckles across his nose looked like a spattering of dark ink, and he swayed as he stood by the ambulance, not thinking to touch its side for support although it was well within reach.

'What? These aren't mine,' Susan told the other nurse, feeling the two vinyl bags suddenly heavy in her arms.

'You brought them on board.'

'Oh, yes, so I did. . .'

'Look after yourself. . .and that doctor of yours. He needs fluids and calories after giving that blood. There's a milk bar across the street.'

'I doubt I'll get him to leave the hospital.'

'Take him to the director of nursing's office. She has a couch, and she won't mind. Get take-away from the milk bar. He gave us 500 ccs and he looks as if he's going to——'

Susan caught Drew just in time. 'I'm all right,' he insisted fuzzily, but his left shoulder was still shored

heavily against her and she had to use all her strength
to help him stand.

'We have to get back to the airport,' Dr Little said
behind them. 'We were on our way to collect two
elderly patients who are coming in for tests when we
were diverted to you, and they'll still be waiting.'

'Go ahead,' Drew managed.

'And thanks,' Susan finished for him.

The director of nursing's office was quiet. Too much
so for Drew, it seemed. He began to prowl around,
shaking his head at Susan's gesture towards the couch,
and then as she saw him sway again she became
insistent.

'Drew, Simon is in surgery. If you want to be still
conscious to see him once he's in Recovery. . .'

'You're right, of course.'

But still she had to push him down, arrange cushions
for him, *forbid* him to move while she left him to go to
the milk bar. It made a change in the pattern of their
relationship. Thinking of the times over the past few
months when his protectiveness towards her had
seemed more of a slight than a compliment, Susan now
saw another side to the issue.

He needs me, and it feels so good to be able to help.
It doesn't matter that he's vulnerable and I'm strong.
Perhaps I shouldn't have minded before when our roles
were reversed. . .

She brought back a container of orange juice, a huge
chocolate milkshake and a hamburger that was greasy
with meat and egg and fried onion on its toasted bun.
Not exactly healthy food, but it would provide the
replenishing carbohydrate and fluid that he needed.
The juice would help to wash down an iron tablet as
well. Perhaps even more importantly, eating and drinking would give him something to do.

Of necessity he was silent as his sensitive mouth
closed around the milkshake's straw, and for the first
time Susan registered just how they both looked. The

white tennis clothes that each still wore were stained
with brown-red patches of blood, and the laces of
Drew's tennis shoes had long ago come undone.
Quietly she leaned forward and tied them for him.

Time passed, the milkshake disappeared, his colour
improved a little, and she finally thought to check the
overnight bags. One was hers, although she hadn't
even recognised it before, and it contained a sunny
beach towel rolled around her still damp swimsuit as
well as the slip of black cocktail dress and its shoes and
accessories. What it *didn't* contain were the more
casual clothes for the barbecue, but it was scarcely
possible to be annoyed with Elaine Hamilton about the
oversight in the circumstances.

The other bag had Simon's and Drew's things in it,
and she said to the doctor gently, 'Here. You should
change. You don't want to go into Recovery all covered
in blood. I'm going to find a bathroom and change
too.'

'Thanks.' He took the clothes from her absently, and
she knew that ninety-five per cent of his attention was
still with Simon. Being a doctor, he would be imagining
each step of the surgery in detail, and thinking to
himself, Now they'll be intubating him. . . By now they
might be cleaning the wound. . . I wonder if they'll
need a graft. . .?

'Do you want me to see if there's a shower?' she
asked him.

'No. . .'

Once the door had closed—so gently—behind Susan,
Drew made the tremendous effort needed to rouse
himself from the paralysing and weakening fear he felt
over Simon. The child was fully his at last, and mixed
with a complex and quite terrifying elation was the
even more terrifying and very superstitious dread that
he would lose his son completely before he had known
any of the joy he wanted to feel.

It *shouldn't* be a difficult surgery. The blood loss,

although dramatic, was no longer life-threatening now that blood—his own blood—and plasmas were available. But with surgery you could never tell. There was that one in ten thousand chance of complications from anaesthesia. There was the chance that he himself had missed some tell-tale sign when he had diagnosed the injury as a relatively simple one. There was, however small, the chance of human error in the operating theatre.

Rising restlessly to his feet, he tore off the stained tennis clothes and climbed into pale olive khaki trousers and a co-ordinating geometric-patterned shirt, tucking in tails and changing shoes and socks automatically. He even combed his hair. But his heart and mind were with Simon all the time. . .

And with Susan. God, it had been good to have her with him today, so quietly contained, not burdening his sizzling brain with one superfluous word, not mouthing any ridiculous formulas of comfort and optimism. Incredible how she could be both a part of all this and yet keep her distance, not trespass too far, respect the fact that this was *his* life.

No! Hey! Hang on! He revolted against this last thought. Damn it! It has to be *her* life, too! I *need* her! He remembered Kate's urging a week ago. Only that? It seemed much longer. Her warning that Susan Carstairs was by no means sitting on a plate awaiting his pleasure. . .

And now, at last, he knew no doubts about what he wanted to do.

'You can come and see him now,' a comfortably plump nurse told Drew and Susan a short while later. The latter felt awkward in her party gear. It was inappropriate, with its slim straps that bared her shoulders and flattered her long neck, but it was better than that badly stained tennis dress.

'Is he awake?' Drew was saying.

'Just. Very groggy. He'll need a lot of rest. . .and he needs to see you. He'll be disoriented. . .but of course you'd know that.'

'Susan, are you coming?' Drew turned to her.

'If. . .if you want me to.'

'I want you to.' The words were low and infused with an intense weight of meaning that made her heart pound although she didn't dare to wonder why the moment should be so significant.

He took her hand in both of his and squeezed it with a pressure that was almost painful, yet still had the power to send a tingle of awareness along her spine. He was standing so close, and she wanted him closer. . .

'Let's go,' she managed.

The small hospital had no fully staffed recovery ward. Instead a quiet alcove just beyond the two operating theatres provided a place where Simon's emergence from anaesthesia could be carefully monitored. Drew bent over the still white-faced boy and stroked some hair away from his forehead. 'Simon?'

Eyelids fluttered and opened drowsily. 'Daddy. . .' A smile softened the childish face and the eyes closed again. It was enough.

'Everything's looking good,' the nurse said. 'We should have him in the ward in half an hour.'

The general surgeon who had operated came up to Drew and they talked technicalities for a few minutes. Susan followed but didn't contribute. Drew's questions were detailed, and the answer to each one seemed to relax and reassure him a little further. The surgery had gone well. The leg should ultimately recover its function completely. When the other doctor left, Drew turned to her. 'Let Simon know that you're here too,' he suggested quietly.

'I don't want to wake him again. . .'

But she had touched the soft hair and small, gently curled fingers before she'd even finished speaking, overtaken by a sweet, rather painful and very powerful tenderness that she didn't fully understand.

Maternal. That was the word for it, and she had no right to feel maternal about Simon. Once again the child stirred, opened his eyes briefly and smiled, but then he drifted off again and Susan straightened. No sense in trying to coax any further response from him. The moment had made her too vulnerable already. This was Drew's son, with Drew's blood literally running in his veins. . .

Catching the direction of Drew's gaze, she saw that he was watching her and immediately she flushed with embarrassment, as if he had caught her half unclothed.

'What's wrong?' she blurted, with a momentary return of all the old awkwardness she had known so often in Melbourne.

'Nothing. . .'

'I know my dress looks a bit silly in a hospital, but Elaine must have mislaid my other clothes,' she gabbled inanely.

'It doesn't look silly. It looks just right for dinner out.'

'Dinner out?' she could only echo.

'Yes. Aren't you hungry?'

'Actually. . .' A clock on the wall told her that it was eight o'clock, a meaningless number after all that had happened, but it *did* provide some clue as to the reason for the hollow stomach she now noticed for the first time.

'There's a Chinese place about ten minutes' walk away, apparently. The Golden Wok. Unless you fancy the hamburgers at that milk bar, and from experience I can't recommend them. . .'

She laughed, responding to the lazy irony in his tone and feeling ridiculously relieved and warmed at his change of mood. During Simon's crisis, she had lived every heartbeat with Drew, and it was so good at last to see that forehead uncreased above his emerald-green eyes, those lips softened, the tan and colour in his cheeks returned.

Outside it was dark, but the air was still warm and it smelled of the sea—salty and fresh, after the dry, indefinable fragrance of the desert. They could even see the sea, Susan realised. Or rather the small estuary that the town had grown around. Odd to think that just a few hours ago she had been five hundred kilometres from the ocean. . .

'I have a son,' Drew said suddenly in the darkness. 'I have a son. . .'

'It's pretty miraculous,' Susan answered.

'And do you know the most miraculous thing? It doesn't make a difference—not to how much I love him.'

'Just to how comfortable it is to feel that love?' Susan suggested quietly.

'Yes. So comfortable. That's an important ingredient of love, isn't it? With Lisa, I never realised that. I thought that love was being on tenterhooks the whole time, fighting and making truces, never really being relaxed. But with you. . .'

'With me?' Hadn't they been talking about Simon? Her heart began to beat strangely.

'With you, Susan,' he repeated, very seriously. 'It's taken me a long time. Kate said it would serve me right if you didn't wait. . .and then I wondered if you'd ever been waiting at all. I had no good reason to think. . . So now I *am* on tenterhooks! Put me out of my misery, please!'

'Drew, *what* are you trying to tell me?' she laughed, hardly daring to understand him.

They had stopped in the middle of the rough gravel path that bordered the quiet street and he was looking down at her, his eyes searching and his words tumbling out as he first caressed her shoulders then drew her so close that she could feel his heart beating in his chest— unless it was *her* heart jumping like that.

'I love you,' he told her. 'Simple. It sounds so simple to me at last and oh, it feels so good to say it!'

'Does it?' she whispered. 'I wonder. . .' His mouth brushed hers as she spoke, then he pulled her still closer.

'Try it, Susan. Go on. . .' he murmured against her lips.

'I never have. . .'

'I know. That's something precious to me. I promise I won't ever forget to cherish that.'

'Then. . .'

'Listen, it's very easy. I. . .love. . .you.'

'I love you.'

'There. . . Doesn't that feel better?'

'It feels very good.'

'And what about, Yes, I will marry you? Do you think you could try that one as well?'

'I think I might, in the right circumstances.'

'And what might they be?'

'Now. . .'

But somehow the words never got said, or, if they did, they were so drowned in a kiss that no one heard them. And it was probably fortunate that Pendleton was a quiet town, because a ten-minute walk to the Chinese restaurant stretched effortlessly into half an hour under the onslaught of Drew's bold yet gentle mouth, and if anyone had been watching. . .

When finally they did arrive, the Golden Wok was thrown into unaccustomed kitchen chaos at the sight of two new diners so late—for this town—in the evening, but Drew and Susan didn't care what they ate. They didn't care that they hadn't booked into a motel, either, although both the places in Pendleton closed their doors to new arrivals promptly at eleven.

Susan had never been so hazy about time in her life, and Drew was wondering what kind of dress would do his bride justice—a sophisticated creation from an expensive wedding boutique in Perth, or some simple

thing in Swiss cotton and lace that Margaret Latham
would run up on her machine from a pattern she and
Susan had pored over. Something that showed off her
slim neck and courageous shoulders, something that
didn't swamp those delicately crafted features—the
arched eyebrows, the perfect bow of her lips.

My God, I've been in love with her since Melbourne,
he decided very happily and very extravagantly. But
perhaps I'd better not admit that today. . .

Susan, longing for him to finish that spring roll so
that she could kiss him again, was giddily thinking
exactly the same thing.

MILLS & BOON

Christmas Treasures

Unwrap the romance this Christmas

Four exciting new Romances by favourite Mills & Boon
authors especially for you this Christmas.

A Christmas Wish - Betty Neels
Always Christmas - Eva Rutland
Reform Of The Rake - Catherine George
Christmas Masquerade - Debbie Macomber

Published: November 1994

Cruel Legacy

One man's untimely death deprives a wife of her husband, robs a man of his job and offers someone else the chance of a lifetime...

Suicide — the only way out for Andrew Ryecart, facing crippling debt. An end to his troubles, but for those he leaves behind the problems are just beginning, as the repercussions of this most desperate of acts reach out and touch the lives of six different people — changing them forever.

Special large-format paperback edition

OCTOBER
£8.99

W⬤RLDWIDE

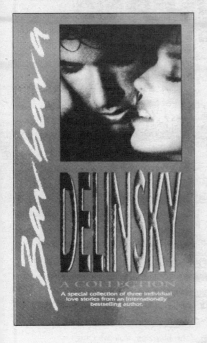

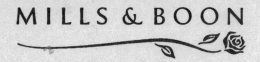

MILLS & BOON

LOVE ON CALL

The books for enjoyment this month are:

LAKESIDE HOSPITAL Margaret Barker
A FATHER'S LOVE Lilian Darcy
PASSIONATE ENEMIES Sonia Deane
BURNOUT Mary Hawkins

♥ ♥ ♥ ♥ ♥

Treats in store!

Watch next month for the following absorbing stories:

ONCE MORE, WITH FEELING Caroline Anderson
HEART ON THE LINE Jean Evans
NO ALTERNATIVE Josie Metcalfe
A DIFFERENT DESTINY Meredith Webber